A VANISHED HAND

A Vanished Hand

and Others

by

Clotilde Graves
("Richard Dehan")

Swan River Press
Dublin, Ireland
MMXXI

A Vanished Hand
by Clotilde Graves

Published by
Swan River Press
Dublin, Ireland
October MMXXI

www.swanriverpress.ie
brian@swanriverpress.ie

Introduction © Melissa Edmundson
This edition © Swan River Press

Dust jacket design by Meggan Kehrli
from artwork © Brian Coldrick

Typeset in Garamond by Steve J. Shaw

Published with assistance from Dublin UNESCO
City of Literature and Dublin City Libraries

ISBN 978-1-78380-756-7

Swan River Press published
a limited hardback edition of
A Vanished Hand in October 2021.

Contents

Introduction

The life and work of Clotilde Graves crosses many boundaries. She was born in Ireland and acknowledged within herself what she called "a good deal of the Irish fighting-blood". Yet only a few of her many novels and short stories contain any directly identifiable Irish content. She also existed between two distinct identities. During her early life and the years she spent in the theatre world, Graves was known professionally as "Clo Graves". However, as her career as a fiction writer became more established, she adopted the persona of "Richard Dehan", novelist and story writer. She often even signed her letters "Richard Dehan/Clotilde Graves". Her appearance also moved between established gender norms. Magazines identified her as a "Bohemian" who dressed in male attire, wore short hair, and smoked in public. Her writing is likewise varied and comprises several different genres. Throughout her decades as an author, Graves wrote over fifteen plays, nearly twenty novels, and around two hundred short stories. The majority of these stories do not feature fantastical content, but Graves remained devoted to such stories from her first collection to her last.

The relative scarcity of these types of stories within her impressively varied oeuvre mean that it has been easy for Graves's work in the genre to be overlooked compared to her contemporaries. In many ways, the output of her fellow countrywoman, Katharine Tynan (1859-1931), provides a good comparison. Both writers frequently delved into the otherworldly in their short fiction, but neither identified as—or were widely recognised as—writers of ghost stories. This, in turn, meant that Graves's work remained underappreciated within the wider genres of Gothic, weird, and supernatural fiction. Although a few of her stories have been included in anthologies over the years, Graves's work has gone largely unnoticed, even among recently published collections of women's supernatural writing. Compounding this problem is the relative scarcity of the original collections themselves. While some of these books have been digitised, others exist in only a few print copies, making it difficult for her work to find a wider audience. This collection seeks to recover Graves's fantastical writing by including stories from across her career, stories which challenge definition and skilfully blend genres. Within the following pages, readers will find traditional ghost stories, weird tales, science fictions, fantasies, and forays into horror.

Clotilde Inez Augusta Mary Graves was born on 3 June 1863 at the Barracks, in Buttevant, Co. Cork. She was the third daughter of Major William H. Graves, of the Eighteenth Royal Irish Regiment, and Antoinette Deane Graves, of Harwich. Like her father, Graves's mother descended from a military family. She was the daughter of Captain George Anthony Deane and was related to Admiral Sir Anthony Deane, a naval architect and master shipwright during the reign of Charles II. On her paternal side, she was related to the Irish poet and folklorist Alfred Perceval Graves (1846-1931), who was the father of the poet and classicist Robert Graves. When Clotilde was nine years old, the family moved to England and settled in Southsea. During this early period of her life, she gathered much of her knowledge of military and naval life that she would later use to great effect in her fiction. At the age of twelve, she wrote a burlesque version of Tennyson's *Idylls of the King* and acted it out with her siblings in the garret of the family home. According to Clodagh Finn in *Through Her Eyes* (2019), Graves was largely self-educated and spent much time in a family friend's library voraciously reading. Her own library would eventually include some four thousand books.

Graves attended the Royal Female School of Art in Bloomsbury, London. To support herself, she worked in the British Museum galleries and as a journalist, writing and drawing sketches for the comic magazines *Fun* and *Judy*. Eventually, she decided to pursue her dream of becoming a playwright. Over the course of five years, she took minor parts as a member of a touring theatre company in order to gain experience. Graves admitted that she was not suited for an acting career, though, and said in a 21 February 1900 interview for *The Sketch*: "I was a wretchedly poor actress, and was always better able to play anybody else's part than my own" ("A Chat with Miss Clo Graves"). Graves claimed that her real "gift" was as a stage manager.

In the 1890s, Graves lived as a lodger on Redesdale Street in Chelsea and listed her profession as "journalist". By 1901, she was living on England's Lane in Haverstock Hill in Hampstead, London, and then moved to Orchardleigh, Warborough, Wallingford, Berkshire. According to papers in the Royal Literary Fund archives, Graves experienced financial difficulties throughout the first decade of the century. Friends and former employers wrote letters in support of her application for assistance, and these letters give insight into Graves's life during this time. They mention her continuing ill health and the fact that she was forced to support relatives. These letters stress that her situation is due to circumstances beyond her control. They also describe Graves's professionalism and her talent as a writer. These issues are summed up by Sir Sidney Colvin (then working as Keeper of Prints and Drawings at the British Museum) in a 26 January 1905 letter to the fund's secretary, Arthur Llewelyn Roberts: "Miss Graves is a writer of great industry and no mean talent. She has supported indigent relatives for many years, and is cordially respected by all who know her." By the 1920s, she had moved to The Towers, Beeding, Sussex. During the final decades of her life, she suffered from chronic poor health (including several attacks of double pneumonia) and spent sixteen years in a wheelchair. Graves had converted to Catholicism in 1896 and near the end of her life, moved to the Convent of Lourdes, Oxhey Lane, Hatch End, Middlesex. In 1931, the year before her death, she received a civil list pension in the amount of £100 in recognition of her literary work. She died at the convent on 3 December 1932.

In many ways, Graves lived an unconventional life for a Victorian and Edwardian-era woman. An obituary in New Zealand's *Evening Post* noted: "She wore short hair and affected a masculine manner and cut of costume, and smoked cigarettes in public some 35 years ago, when such characteristics were considered eccentric" (14 January 1933). She never married and lived alone for most of her adult life. In a 1900 interview, she called the many books that lined the walls of her study her "companions". Her hobbies included gardening, cycling, driving, angling, and coin collecting. This progressive attitude often translated into her journalism. For instance, in her article "Employment for Girls: Chromo-Lithography", which appeared in the May 1888 issue of the girl's monthly magazine *Atalanta* (then edited by L. T. Meade), she begins by addressing the disadvantages placed on young women who wish to pursue professional opportunities:

> What shall we do with our boys? is a question which
> has been reiterated by anxious parents and guardians
> for centuries past. What shall we do with ourselves?
> cry the girls of this our nineteenth century. How
> shall we find out what especial talents are ours, so as
> to develop them? For what profession or trade shall
> we qualify ourselves from the very beginning so that
> if our destinies are not fulfilled by marriage we may
> never find ourselves hopelessly stranded on the iron-
> bound shores of impecunious spinsterhood?

She contributed many fiction and non-fiction pieces to
major periodicals of the day, including *Punch*, *Judy* (under
the pseudonym "The Hurdy Gurdy Man"), *The World*, *The
Penny Illustrated Paper*, *The Sketch*, *The Sporting Times*, *The
Illustrated London News*, *The Pall Mall Gazette*, *St. James's
Gazette*, and *Lady's Pictorial*, among others. Her first play,
the five-act tragedy *Nitocris*, was performed in Drury Lane
in 1887. The following year, she wrote the lyrics for the
pantomime of *Puss in Boots*. Also in 1888, Graves co-wrote
(along with Edward Rose and William Sydney) an adaptation
of H. Rider Haggard's 1887 novel *She*, which was performed
at the Gaiety Theatre. On 22 August 1888, the *Dublin
Evening Mail* hinted at Clotilde Graves's growing popularity:

> Miss Graves, or, as she is familiarly termed, "Clo
> Graves," is very versatile in her genius. She is a
> dramatist, a novel writer, a burlesque poet, an
> artist, and has even worked at stereotyping her own
> sketches. Introductions to her charming chambers in
> Henrietta Street, Covent Garden, are much sought
> for by the literary Bohemians of Fleet Street. Not
> to know Clo Graves is to argue oneself unknown in
> literary and Press circles. ("London Letter")

This success continued throughout the 1890s with the plays *Rachel* (performed in 1890 at the Haymarket Theatre), *Dr. and Mrs. Neill* (which debuted at the Theatre Royal in Manchester in 1894), *A Mother of Three* (performed at the Comedy Theatre in 1896), *The Bishop's Eye* (which debuted at the Vaudeville Theatre in 1900), and *The Bond of Ninon* (produced at the Savoy in 1906). Graves collaborated with the actress Gertrude Kingston on *A Matchmaker*, performed at the Shaftesbury Theatre in 1896, as well as with Lady Colin Campbell on *St. Martin's Summer*, which was staged in Brighton in 1902. She was also an active member of the Theatrical Ladies' Guild.

Clotilde Graves started publishing books in the late 1880s (often under the name "Clo Graves"), with her earliest titles being comedic works for the "Judy Office", an offshoot of *Judy* magazine published in London by Gilbert Dalziel. These include *The Belle of Rock Harbour* (1887) and *The Pirate's Hand* (1889). *The Lovers' Battle*, based on Alexander Pope's *The Rape of the Lock*, was published by Grant Richards in 1902. Her novels published in the 1890s, such as *Maids in a Market Garden* (1894) and *A Well-Meaning Woman* (1896), contain feminist overtones with issues surrounding women in the workplace, women's suffrage, and choosing to remain single. In *Maids in a Market Garden*, the protagonist Octavia Wall is loosely based on the social reformer Octavia Hill. According to Jenny Bloodworth in her 2012 doctoral thesis on Graves, these novels represent Graves's focus on writing "predominately for a female readership, furnishing them with tales that were set, sometimes, within a broader scope than just the traditional private sphere but which, typically, featured a range of strong, independent-minded women". She also contributed chapters to multi-author collections such as *The Fate of Fenella* (1892), which included pieces from Arthur Conan Doyle and Bram Stoker, as well as the opening chapter to *Seven Xmas Eves* (1894).

With the publication of *The Dop Doctor* (1910), Graves shifted to even more ambitious subject matter. *The Dop Doctor* is a realistic, and at times unflinching, depiction of the Boer War. It was Graves's first bestseller, ran through forty reprintings, and was adapted into a 1915 film directed by Fred Paul. It is set alternatively in England and in South Africa's Transvaal during the Second Boer War (1899-1902), particularly the siege of Mafeking, and focuses on a number of characters, including Owen Saxham, a disgraced doctor who redeems himself during the war, and Lynette Mildare, an abused orphan who is rescued by nuns. This novel is significant because it is the first time Graves used the pseudonym "Richard Dehan", the name that would appear on all her future books. In his chapter on Clotilde Graves in *When Winter Comes to Main Street* (1922), one of the few extended contemporary studies of her life and career, Grant Overton describes how "Richard Dehan" became a separate personality. Overton notes that she signed her personal letters "Richard Dehan" first, followed by "Clotilde Graves", who became "a secondary personality". He speculates that, like many women writers of the period, Graves turned to a male pseudonym because a war novel "required a man's signature". Yet Overton also observes that the name—however necessary it might have been—gave Graves the freedom to write on a wide variety of topics:

> There is no final disassociation between Clotilde Graves and Richard Dehan. Richard Dehan, novelist, steadily employs the material furnished in valuable abundance by Clotilde Graves's life [. . .] Born of necessity and opportunity and a woman's

inventiveness, Richard Dehan took over whatever of Clotilde Graves's he could use. He is now the master. [. . . .] Clotilde Graves—but she does not matter. I think she existed to bring Richard Dehan into the world. ("Alias Richard Dehan")

Though Overton oversimplifies the dynamic between author and literary persona, he does give a sense of the importance of the persona to Graves as a writer. The name change allowed her to fully embody the life of a professional author as she imagined it to be while also inhabiting the social and professional freedoms enjoyed by men of the period. Perhaps we could say that in "Richard Dehan", Graves achieved her greatest and most successful role.

Graves's own thoughts on this decision to change her professional name can be found in a brief reminiscence included in *William Heinemann: A Memoir* (1928). She recalls meeting with Heinemann and his partner Sydney Pawling in their offices before the publication of *The Dop Doctor*. Both Heinemann and Pawling questioned why she would want to drop her name given the fact that critics and readers alike had become so familiar with "Clotilde Graves":

So had the owner of the name in question, now approaching her fiftieth summer, and when Sydney Pawling had rumbled objections in his deep, melodious bass, and William Heinemann, fixing me with his gleaming spectacles, had added to the force of his expostulations the rapid gestures of his supple, darting hands, I had no more convincing argument to put forward than that I had known Clotilde Graves for a long time, and regarded her and her attainments with a certain proprietorial esteem, but that I was more than a little bored with her, and that I would like to drop her for a while.

She then relates a story about Patrick Brontë giving his shy daughters a mask through which to speak their minds, urging them to converse boldly because no one could see them. This, to Graves, was what she wanted for herself:

> Perhaps the *nom de guerre* I had chosen was to serve as my mask when the thoughts, reflections, experiences and griefs of a life-time, contained between the battered leaves of eighty-seven notebooks and wrought into the chapters of a novel, should be sent out into the world. I had written articles and stories and verses and plays, but the book I had entitled *The Dop Doctor* was another matter. This time I had filled my fountain-pen from the veins of my heart!

The success of *The Dop Doctor* led William Heinemann to publish several more works by Graves under the name "Richard Dehan". These subsequent novels included *Between Two Thieves* (1912), a narrative about Florence Nightingale (through the character Ada Merling) set during the Crimean War; *The Man of Iron* (1915), about the Franco-Prussian War; *That Which Hath Wings* (1918), a novel about aviation during the First World War; and *The Just Steward* (1922), a story which moves from ancient Rome to modern times. Heinemann also published the majority of Graves's short fiction, which she brought out in quick succession. These include *The Headquarter Recruit* (1913), *The Cost of Wings* (1914), *Off Sandy Hook* (1915), *Earth to Earth* (1916), *Under the Hermés* (1917), *A Sailor's Home* (1919), *The Eve of Pascua* (1920), and *The Villa of the Peacock* (1921). Two later collections, *The Man with the*

Mask (1931) and *The Third Graft* (1933), were published by Thornton Butterworth and John Long, respectively. Her novels of the 1920s and 1930s include *The Pipers of the Market Place* (1924), *The Sower of the Wind* (1927), *The Lovers of the Market-Place* (1928), *Shallow Seas* (1930), and *Dead Pearls* (1932).

Clotilde Graves's collections of short fiction received generally positive reviews. Reviewers found her stories entertaining and varied in their subject matter. Upon the publication of *The Headquarter Recruit*, the *Review of Reviews* wrote in July 1913: "The stories here given to the public are models of what short stories should be— never banal, never wholly sentimental, yet with sentiment cropping up in an unexpected way, unconventional and virile." Many remarked upon Graves's ability to effectively blend genres in her writing, from romance to tragedy, and adventure to comedy. *The Saturday Review* called *The Cost of Wings* "agreeably varied" and commented how the "occult" stories blended well with the "wit, humour, pathos and satire" of the other stories in the collection (28 March 1914). The *Review of Reviews* likewise remarked that each of the twenty-six stories was "so entirely different" and "pictured with the vivid brush, which makes them live in the memory" (April 1914). In October 1917, *The Bookman* recommended *Under the Hermés* and noted that Graves's work in the short story matched her talent for longer fiction. In June 1931, writing about *The Man with the Mask*, *The Bookman* was still praising her ability to craft a good story, writing, "She can tell a love story and describe a rough-and-tumble with equal skill, and she has a sure touch both in pathos and in humour."

For two decades, from *The Headquarter Recruit* (1913) to the posthumously published *The Third Graft* (1933), Graves experimented with the Gothic, weird, and supernatural, and all her short fiction collections contain at least one supernatural or weird tale. Graves also excelled at incorporating genre themes into her novella-length work. In "The Man Who Lost Himself", included in *A Sailor's Home* (1919), the protagonist experiments with astral travel and gradually loses his physical ties to Earth. "The Extraordinary Adventures of an Automobile", which appears in *The Villa of the Peacock* (1921), features the spirit of Petrolina, who brings a car to life. In "The Third Graft", the title story of Graves's last collection, a monkey gland experiment performed as an act of revenge gradually brings out the bestial nature of a man.

Clotilde Graves's fantastical stories show a remarkable range of places, plots, and characters. As contemporary reviewers noted, no two stories are the same, and this is equally true of her genre fiction. The tales in this collection range from ghost stories to science fiction, horror, and fantasy. There are stories with a theatrical flair that concern obsession, betrayal, and revenge, as well as more intimate stories that examine the effects of grief and loss.

As difficult as writing an effective ghost story is, Graves goes a step further by combining the supernatural with another notoriously difficult genre: comedy. And indeed, Graves is responsible for some of the best humorous ghost stories ever written. This quality was appreciated by contemporary reviewers who frequently highlighted her more amusing tales. For instance, in November 1913, *The Bookman* reviewer for *The Headquarter Recruit* called "Clairvoyance" "deliciously humorous". Often humour in Gothic fiction takes aim at itself by targeting its own tropes and stereotypes. Such humour represents the playfulness of a genre that never takes itself too seriously. Within Irish literature, Graves's contributions to the humorous Gothic tale are part of an older tradition that includes Joseph

Sheridan Le Fanu's stories "The Ghost and the Bone-setter" (1838) and "The Quare Gander" (1840), both of which treat the supernatural through a comedic lens, as well as Oscar Wilde's "The Canterville Ghost" (1887). In *Gothic and the Comic Turn* (2005), Avril Horner and Sue Zlosnik argue that the "comic Gothic" highlights the hybridity of the Gothic mode. They note that in addition to being texts that entertain, comic Gothic narratives can also address serious issues, yet in a more detached way than realistic tales. This "detachment" can sometimes catch us off guard when darker elements are introduced into a Gothic narrative.

Indeed, many of Graves's stories tread a fine line between comedy and tragedy, and often we are not sure whether to laugh at the characters or cry at their misfortunes. This quality in Graves's writing is a direct result of her theatrical background and in many stories we see Clotilde the playwright at work. There is a farcical element to Graves's early stories, but this tendency is frequently undercut by something more serious. For instance, the comic absurdity of the circus parents in "Peter" (1917) is perfectly balanced with the unhappiness and despair of their mistreated son. The foolish ignorance of the adults is put into direct contrast with the knowing cynicism of the boy. In this brief story, Graves expertly manages the reader's emotions.

In "The Compleat Housewife" (1910), Graves plays with the trope of the ancestral ghost whose attachment to her book of household management makes her a supernatural Mrs. Beeton. In a twist on the typical haunted house tale, the American Lydia Randolph, new bride to Sir Bryan Corbryan and mistress of Hindway Abbey, hopes that the resident ghost, Lady Deborah, will be a companion and teach her to become a proper English lady. However, Lady Deborah has other plans and wants to leave the house by any means necessary. She reassures Lydia that she has arranged for other ghosts to take her place because "a family residence without a ghost" would be disreputable:

> "Sir Umphrey, who got grant of the demesne from King Henry VIII, and, as you may have heard, murdered the abbot who took exception to the grant, has arranged to haunt the inhabited wings as well as the shut-up portion. You have also a third share in a banshee brought into the family by one of the Desmonds, who intermarried with us in 1606, and there is a hugely impressive death-watch in the wainscoting of your room."

The comedic exchanges between the young bride and Lady Deborah are accompanied by the recipe for an extravagant meat pie that has proved fatal to a past member of the Corbryan family. This leaves readers to wonder if Graves is also remarking upon the pursuit of domestic perfection and how such pursuits can ultimately prove harmful.

In addition to their levity, the stories in this collection often address underlying social concerns as Graves, like many women writers of the time, used the supernatural as a form of critique. Women's issues frequently surface in these stories. Amongst the humour in "Clairvoyance" (1913) Graves manages to interject some social commentary as the male protagonist laments how women seem to be in every profession, meaning that there will be "[n]othing for the men to do soon". Miss Predicta herself makes a good living as a fraudulent spirit medium, representing yet another profession that allowed women to support themselves. The story hinges on miscommunication between the spirit medium and the sitter as the messages Miss Predicta receives from the "other side" are misinterpreted to comic effect.

"A Vanished Hand" (1914) is a ghost story with an underlying message about women as material objects. The woman in question is both a possession and possessing. Through the ghost, Graves raises concerns over how women, particularly women as artistic muses, are used and eventually discarded when they become useless or inconvenient. This is summed up by the unnamed woman:

> "Only the dead are faithful to Love—because they are dead," she said. "The living live on—and forget! They may remember sometimes to regret us—beat their breasts and call upon our names—but they shudder if we answer back across the distance; and if we should offer to come back, 'Return!' they say; 'go and lie down in the comfortable graves we have made you; there is no room for you in your old places any more!'"

The regret experienced in this story is directly tied to the choices one makes, choices—like death—that cannot be undone.

"How the Mistress Came Home" (1914) is a more traditional ghost story with a twist ending. A family curse comes into play and issues of inheritance, ownership, and property are examined through the figure of the ghost. Graves wisely leaves the exact reason for the curse to the reader's imagination, focusing instead on the ghost's experience. Lady Wroth's response to Mrs. Ansdey about not believing in ghosts might indeed echo how Graves felt about her fictional ghosts:

Not in ghosts as they are commonly imagined; those shadowy white things that point and scare and hover [. . .] but in the spirits of the departed—it may be long-dead, or newly called from earth—who borrow for a little while the semblance in which they lived and loved, and return for one last look at a beloved home, or come for one dear glimpse of what might, but for the Infinite Eternal Will, have been a home. You believe in them, do you not?

In this passage, we see the author's desire to broaden the tradition of ghost stories. Her ghosts always have a purpose and seek to reconnect to a lost home and a past that is unattainable. Both her living characters and her ghostly ones exist together in these stories and the balance between the two is vital for their respective plots. We become invested in the lives—and deaths—of these people whose motives, desires, and regrets drive the action of the narratives. Graves's first love was the theatre, and she used the skills of a performer and playwright to great effect in her short fiction. As we read these stories, it is as if we are seeing them on the stage—even her ghosts are full of life and energy.

"A Spirit Elopement" (1915) is another example where Graves plays with the traditional tropes of the ghost story. Like "Clairvoyance", this story is a comedic take on spiritualism and the consequences of forming attachments with those on the "other side". Relationships (good and bad) are always at the heart of Clotilde Graves's stories and "A Spirit Elopement" is a creative approach to examining how those relationships grow and change—in life and in death.

Graves moved beyond the domestic ghost story as well. "The Tooth of Tuloo" (1917) takes place in the Arctic regions and is a quest fantasy involving Inuit traditions. In order to prove himself, Kolosha, the young hero, must undertake a dangerous journey to the Island of the Four Winds in order to retrieve a magical tooth from the undead mummy Tuloo. The story showcases Graves's interest in remote regions of the world while exhibiting her ability to craft a narrative full of action and comic episodes. The story is another example of Graves's skill at writing effective dialogue, a talent that she undoubtedly transferred from playwrighting to fiction.

For other stories, Graves enters the realm of science fiction. "Lady Clanbevan's Baby" (1915) and "Lilium Peccatorum" (1916) combine elements of experimental science within domestic settings. The former story involves a scientist who experiments with radium in order to achieve eternal youth. At the time of the story's publication, radium had recently been discovered by Marie and Pierre Curie and the radioactive properties of the chemical element fascinated the public (often to lethal effect). The potential uses for radium—which during Graves's time seemed limitless—provide the plot for the story and adds a layer of suspense as the narrator uncovers Lady Clanbevan's secret. In "Lilium Peccatorum", an evil plant—the "Sin Lilly"—has unforeseen consequences on the actions of its new owners. The pacing and characterisation are always on point as Graves effortlessly moves her characters around like players on a chessboard. She even has one of the protagonists remark that the events are like a "rotten play". Like many of her literary forebears in the nineteenth century who considered the negative effects of scientific experimentation through the lens of the Gothic and supernatural, Graves seems to be warning her readers that advances in science can be useful, but they can also be destructive and deadly in the hands of desperate people.

Introduction

"The Great Beast of Kafue" (1917) imagines a world where prehistoric creatures are still living in remote jungles. The life of the story's creature is threatened when colonial invaders discover the secret of the beast's existence, something known and respected by Indigenous people for centuries. "The Great Beast of Kafue" is also a double-edged story. The fantasy and wonder of imagining that a dinosaur could still exist in a modern world is subtly undercut by a devastatingly real fact: the narrator's unrelenting guilt over the part he may have played in his wife's death. His decision not to kill the beast at the end of the story is one of bitterness, not of pity. The losses experienced by beast and man coincide in the story. The narrator ensures that the beast will continue to mourn the loss of its mate the same way he is forced to mourn his wife.

"The Mother of Turquoise" (1907) is an adventure tale with a supernatural twist and showcases Graves's ability to craft an entertaining, well-paced narrative. Supernatural events are a driving force of the plot and uncover the strengths and weaknesses of the characters in their respective unfamiliar and dangerous environments. "The Mother of Turquoise" rivals the best adventure stories of the era. Like many such stories, it is a study in the effects of colonialism, though the more progressive tendencies in Graves's writing are sometimes marred by instances of Eurocentric viewpoints and negative descriptions of Indigenous people. (Another example appears in an excerpt included by Overton in his chapter on Graves that follows the stories in this volume.) Through the narrator's eyes, readers see how the promise of material wealth negatively affects the young protagonist to the point where he gives up his privileged education and professional opportunities, which place him in a position to help people, in order to pursue personal gain. Like "The Great Beast of Kafue", the colonists are

xxiii

overwhelmed by the supernatural power that exists in the particular region, a power that is better understood by the Indigenous people who suffer at the hands of the outsiders. Though the respective supernatural entities are left to live in "Kafue" and are killed in "Turquoise", there is a sense of waste and loss that pervades each story as Graves eschews a "neat" ending in favour of moral ambiguity.

The mood becomes darker and more serious as readers move from Graves's earlier story collections to her later ones. The levity of the earlier stories is replaced by narratives of loss, obsession, and isolation. These later stories show Graves's treatment of the personal costs and aftermath of war. In "Dark Dawn" (1931), the vision of the ancient Roman soldier seen by the young couple on a remote field in Britain symbolises the never-ending cycle of war and death. The ominous tone of the story begins early and builds to the narrative's inevitable conclusion as Graves is careful to point out how war always demands a sacrifice in the form of the younger generation. "The Friend" (1931) is seen from the perspective of a war widow whose personal loss prevents her from celebrating with others at the return of the soldiers. As with "Peter", Death returns as a character in the story, one who offers hope to the miserable.

Although this collection is by no means comprehensive, it is my hope that *A Vanished Hand and Others* offers readers a wide-ranging selection of some of the best of Clotilde Graves's fantastical fiction. These stories showcase the breadth of range she frequently employed in her writing. We are taken from ancestral British homes to the Arctic regions of the Inuit people, from the jungles of Bulawayo to the deserts of Syria. The characters are just as varied. Circus performers and spirit mediums share space with supernatural creatures that take the forms of adult babies, evil plants, living mummies, prehistoric dinosaurs, Boer War soldiers, and Death itself.

To this selection of stories are added two contemporary pieces related to Graves, both of which give additional insight into her life and career. "Miss Clo Graves at Home", published in *The Gentlewoman* on 2 May 1896, is one of the few interviews Graves granted and provides an informative personal account of her early interest in writing and performing, her move to London, and her success as a playwright. Grant Overton's chapter "Alias Richard Dehan" originally appeared in *When Winter Comes to Main Street* (1922), a survey of recommended authors whose works were published in America by George H. Doran. The chapter represents one of the few extended studies of Graves's life and work published during her lifetime and considers how the persona of "Richard Dehan" functioned for Graves both personally and professionally.

Clotilde Graves, with her own need to push boundaries in her personal and professional life, was well-suited to write in the Gothic mode, an area of literature that itself is notorious for blurring boundaries. She was able to write equally well about both the lighter and darker aspects of life, a quality that the *Irish Examiner* noted was a distinct part of her Irishness. Graves "was Irish not only by birth in Buttevant, but in her gift of humour and sense of 'the tears of things'." (6 December 1932)

In a 31 January 1905 letter to Llewelyn Roberts, the journalist and editor Sidney Low said of Graves:

> There was a literary quality about her articles which is too rare among writers for the press: and I always felt that if Miss Graves had been able to release herself from the stress of constant journalism, she would

have produced imaginative work of exceptional merit. The impression has been confirmed by many of her short stories and essays, which I have read in magazines and weekly journals. Hastily as I suppose these were composed they seldom lacked a touch of distinction in style and some grace of fancy.

As more of Clotilde Graves/Richard Dehan's life and work is uncovered, modern readers will also be able to appreciate her distinct style and impressive range of subject matter. Her moments of success seemed to always be met with new personal challenges, but writing was one of the few constants in her life. One would hope that the imaginative fiction she wrote allowed her to momentarily escape from life's hardships. It certainly offers us instances of laughter, delight, pathos, and wonder. Though this selection comprises only a small portion of her overall output, Graves's fantastical tales deserve to take their place beside some of the best writing in that genre during the first half of the twentieth century.

Melissa Edmundson
Greenville, South Carolina
August 2021

A Vanished Hand

How the Mistress Came Home

The avenue of lofty elms was veiled in a white fog; upon the low-lying parklands, cropped meadows, and sere stubble-fields, the same woolly vapour lay dankly. But the square windows of the fine old Tudor manor-house flashed with ruddy light, and the hospitable hearth-fires of the hall diffused glow and radiance through open doors. Sir Vivian and Lady Wroth were coming home after a honeymoon of eight months' duration spent in scampering over the face of the habitable globe; and the village was in a state of loyal ferment over the advent of the lord and lady of the manor. Already the local band, heavily primed with home-brewed, was posted at the station in readiness to burst into the strains of "See the Conquering Hero" upon the arrival of the London express. Eight sturdy labourers, in clean smock-frocks, waited, rope in hand, for the opportunity of harnessing themselves to the bridal brougham, while Venetian masts, upbearing strings of flags and fairy lanterns, testified to the strength and temperature of popular good-will.

"A sweet pretty creature, 'm, I hear!" said Mrs. Ansdey, the white-haired, handsome, black-silk clad housekeeper to the Rector's wife, who had driven up to the house to ask for a cup of tea, and leave a parcel addressed to the new mistress of the manor, containing three dozen very raspy cambric handkerchiefs, hemmed and initialled by the Girls' Sewing Class at the National Schools.

"Quite a picture, Sir Vivian's valet said!" added the butler, who was comparatively young, not being over sixty, and therefore looked down upon by Mrs. Ansdey from her vantage of fifteen summers.

"Beauty is grass!" said the Rector's wife, who was not overburdened with the commodity. She was a long, thin, high-nosed woman, with colour distributed over her countenance in little islands. She drank her tea, and toasted her large, useful feet at the glowing wood-fire, and praised the Sally Lunns.

Her reverend partner was down at the village reading-rooms, rehearsing the shrill-voiced schoolchildren in the "Greet Ye To-night, Thrice Happy Pair", chorus from *Lohengrin*. She knew the quality of the cocoa to be obtained there, and longed to share with him the hospitable burden of Mrs. Ansdey's silver tray. But as this amicable division of spoil was manifestly impossible, the Rector's wife consoled herself by making a clean sweep. And so she ate and drank and chatted to the not displeased Mrs. Ansdey with unflagging vigour, while the famous Reynolds portraits of departed ladies of the manor smiled and simpered from the shining panelled walls, and the grey-muzzled bloodhounds, last of a famous race and favourite of the last Baronet, snored upon the leopard-skin hearthrug.

"You have had many visitors this season?" queried the Rector's wife, with a calculating glance at the donation box, the contents of which went to the Cottage Hospital twice in the year.

"Troops of them," returned the housekeeper, nodding her lace lappets. "And, as usual, half of 'em with American twangs. Even if they didn't talk through their noses, I should guess 'em from the States, shouldn't you, Mr. Cradell?"

"Without doubt, ma'am," rejoined the butler. "There's a feverish anxiety to get the greatest amount of information in the shortest possible time, and an equally ardent determination to finger what isn't meant to be fingered, price what can't be priced, and buy what isn't for sale, which, to my mind, is a trademark distinguishing the bearer, male or female, as hailing from the other side of the Atlantic."

"Even if he didn't call me 'marm'—if he's a man and middle-aged, and put American dollars in the box instead of English half-crowns if he happens to be a lady," continued Mrs. Ansdey. "But what I will say is, if it was with my latest breath, that the young ladies are most elegant and have a real appreciation for old and what you might call romantic things," she added somewhat hastily; and the Rector's wife said, as she added sugar to her fourth cup:

"The new Lady Wroth is an American, I have always understood."

"Born in Washington, but educated in Paris," said Mr. Cradell, putting a fresh log of apple-wood upon the glowing fire at the lower end of the hall.

"She comes of a fine old family, we have always understood," said the housekeeper, smoothing her lace apron with her plump white hands. "Rutherford her maiden name was, and with her beauty and her jewels— for her late papa was a Senator, besides being what I've heard called a Railway King—she created a sensation when she was presented by the Duchess of Balgowrie last May but one."

"As to her style of good looks," said Mr. Cradell, dusting lichen from his coat, "Sir Vivian was always partial to dark beauty. 'What is she like?' says he to me when I took the liberty of asking, as an old servant may. 'A black pearl, Cradell, and I hope to wear my jewel in my bonnet as my ancestor Sir Guy wore Queen Elizabeth's ruby—until the day I die!' He'd a light in his eyes when he said it, and what with love and happiness and all, he looked more like a boy of twenty-three than a man of forty. And I said to Mrs. Ansdey, 'If ever there was a love-match,' I says, 'Sir Vivian's is one.' And now the carriage is waiting at the station to bring home both the master and the mistress—bless them both!"

"She wrote to me from Mentone," went on Mrs. Ansdey, "and I truly call it a pretty thought, and a gracious one, of me that have been my master's nurse, and held him on my knees when he picked out bounding 'B' and curly 'Q' with an ivory crotchet-hook." She produced from a Morocco pocket-book, of solid and responsible appearance, a letter written with violet ink on thin foreign paper, in delicate upright characters. "*'My husband has told me of all your faithful service and true devotion to him and his,'*" she read; "*'and I hope before long to take your kind hand in mine and thank you for him and for myself!'*" There now!"

"Gracious and graceful too," said old Cradell, who had beaten noiseless time to the reading of the young mistress's letter with one wrinkled finger on a withered palm. "Good breeding there—and old blood—in every line!"

"And she looks forward to seeing her husband's dear old English home," went on the housekeeper, "and prays God to give them many days in it together—and I trust He will!"

"Let us hope so, for all concerned!" said the Rector's wife, who resented theological references as trenching upon her own particular province.

"Though in this family it's been like a fate, or a doom, or whatever you might please to term it," said Mrs. Ansdey, "that the course of true love, the deeper it was and the truer it was, was always to be broken—not by change or faithlessness of one that loved, but by the hand of death. There was Sir Geoffrey and Lady Euphrasia—hundreds of years back—that were drowned crossing the ford on the ride home from their baby's christening and the baby lived to be Sir Launcelot, whose bride was carried off by the Black Death before the roses on her wedding garland were withered . . . And then there were Sir Alan and Sir Guy, who were both killed in battle within a year of their weddings, and Sir Vivian's great-grandfather, old Sir Vivian, found his young wife dead at her tapestry-frame when he'd crept up quiet to surprise her with his unexpected return from the Embassy to Rome. And Sir Vivian's own dear mother lived but a very few years after the dear child came to comfort her for his father's early loss. But time goes by, and the curse— if it be a curse, as they say it is, brought upon the founder of the family for some secret deed of evil—the curse may have passed over, or worn itself out. What's that?"

"What's what, ma'am?" asked the butler, as Mrs. Ansdey rose in her rustling silks and made a sign for silence.

"I fancied I heard a timid kind of tap on the hall door," said the housekeeper.

"A robin blew against it, perhaps," said the butler. "They're stupid with the frost."

"There was a footstep too," said Mrs. Ansdey, holding up her hand and making her old-fashioned rings gleam and twinkle in the firelight. "At least, if there wasn't, Mr. Cradell, I admit I've been deceived!"

"We'll see, we'll see!" said Cradell, moving to the great oaken door. "It may be a tramp." The handle turned, the massive oak door moved inwards. The fog had thinned, it had grown clearer beyond doors. Within the frame of the massive lintels appeared the glimmering stone steps, a segment of the formal garden, with its black Irish yews, pale marble urns, and cartwheel beds of late flowers, enclosed within borders of box. Beyond the trees reared a sombre barrier, shutting out the sky, and the chill wind of winter drove the dead leaves in swirls and drifts across the melancholy picture. The Rector's wife, thinking of her walk across the park to the Rectory, sniffed and shivered, and the housekeeper motioned to the butler to shut the door.

"For I was mistaken, as you see, and there's not a living soul about, unless it's skulking in the shadow of the trees," she said. "Another cup of tea, or a drop of cheery brandy, ma'am, to keep the bitter air out as you walk home? Though there's no reason you should walk when there's the pony-chair . . . Or perhaps you would rather—" She started. "Call me nervous, or finical, or what you like," she said, peering anxiously through her gold-rimmed spectacles in the direction of the door. "But, if I spoke with my dying breath, there was a tap, and then a pause, and then another tap, as plain as plain could be!"

"Dear me!" The Rector's wife, alarm in her eyes and crumbs on her chin, rose from her chair, dropping her imitation sable boa. "I really believe I heard it too! . . . Had you not better—?"

Cradell shook his old head and clucked softly with his tongue. "The ladies must always have their way!" he said, shuffling on his neatly polished shoes towards the hall door. He opened it, and both the housekeeper and the Rector's wife uttered a simultaneous exclamation of surprise.

For a woman was standing in the moonlight outside. She was of slight form, and wore a wide-brimmed, feathered hat, and the heavy shadow of the portico fell blackly over her, so that she seemed no more than a silhouette with a pale glimmering background. But a delicate perfume stole upon the senses of those who, from within, looked out at her, and when she moved there was the unmistakable frou-frou of silken linings.

"Ma'am—" the butler began.

"I came on before," a sweet plaintive voice said—a voice that was viola-like in its rather thin, but sweet and vibrating quality. "And you must be Cradell."

"*Ma'am?*" the old servant said again, while the Rector's wife and the housekeeper listened with strained anxiety.

"I am Lady Wroth," came in the clear, vibrating tones. "I came on before . . . It does not matter why. There was a slight accident between Greystoke Station and the Elvand Tunnel. Do not be alarmed. Sir Vivian is safe, quite safe," she went on, as agitated exclamations broke from the three listeners. "Indeed only one person was killed, though two or three are injured, and he—my husband—is helping the sufferers. He is always like that, so ready to help, so full of sympathy. . ."

She was now standing in the firelight, whose ruddy glow illumined the slight figure, and drew gleams of crimson and emerald from the jewels at her throat and shone in the depths of her great dark eyes. Her face was of delicate, pearly paleness, her hair had the tints of autumn leaves, and her draperies, too, were of the tints of autumn. She drew off a glove, and her wedding ring, with its diamond keeper, showed upon the slight and pretty hand, as her travelling mantle of velvet trimmed with costly sables fell to the floor.

"Oh, your ladyship!" cried the housekeeper. "What must you think of us—standing here and staring? But as goodness sees us—what with your sudden coming, and the news about the accident, and all—we've lost our heads, me and Mr. Cradell!"

"So very alarming!" said the Rector's wife. "I trust Lady Wroth will excuse what may seem like an intrusion—"

"The intrusion is mine," said the sweet viola-voice. "I should have given warning of my coming, but it was not to be. Oh! the dear house!" She looked with wondering, shining eyes upon the panelled walls, the trophied arms, the noble

9

pictures, and the quaint antique furniture, and between her lips, of the faintest rose, her delicate teeth gleamed like pearls, as her breath came quick and eager. "Vivian's old home . . . Vivian's home, and mine!" she whispered to herself, and laid a hand upon her heart, as though to check its beating.

"I will not intrude," said the Rector's wife. "I will hope for the pleasure of calling, with the Rector, at a more fitting time. Good-night, Lady Wroth."

The Rector's wife had held out her large hand in its cheap glove, but the new mistress of the manor only smiled upon her with vague, wistful sweetness, and did not touch the massive extremity. Whereupon its owner set down Lady Wroth as "proud", and made a mental note to tell the Rector so, as her large feet carried her out of the house and out of the story.

The two old servants exchanged a glance as the slight figure of their mistress moved across the polished floor, strewn with Oriental rugs and skins of wild beasts.

"Would my lady wish to go to her room, or to have some refreshment in the dining-room?" the housekeeper asked.

My lady declined.

"I have no need of anything. I only wish to rest a little and see my husband's home before starting upon a journey," she explained.

"A journey? Dear, gracious me! And your ladyship just fresh from travel, and shaken by an accident and all!" cried Mrs. Ansdey, shaking her lace lappets.

"I am so used to travel," said her ladyship, "though this is the longest journey I have ever taken—or ever shall take!" She smiled upon the two old people, and settled herself in the seat she had chosen, and resting her elbow upon the arm of it, and her pretty chin in her delicate palm, let her sweet shining eyes travel about the place. "All as he described it, yes!" she whispered to herself. "The mullioned windows with the coats of arms, the carved and painted ceiling, the hooded Tudor fireplaces, the arms and the pictures . . . That is the great Gainsborough portrait of Sir Alan's young wife, the girl who died of grief when they brought her husband's *bâton* of Field Marshal to her—won an hour before he was killed in battle. There is the painting by Velásquez of the Wroth who was made Bishop of Toledo. That must be the Vandyck of Lady Marjorie with the deerhound by her side, and there is the Watts picture of Vivian's young mother playing ball with her boy. Ah! what a sweet, sweet child!"

The plaintive voice thrilled and trembled. Tears might not have been far from the shadowy dark eyes, as Lady Wroth rose and moved to the foot of the great staircase, attended by the housekeeper.

"Shall I show you your rooms, my lady?" Mrs. Ansdey began. "The fires are burning beautifully, and everything is quite ready, and I feel sure your ladyship must need rest after—"

"I will rest presently. But what I wish now, is to be shown the house, if you are not too tired. Lady Audrey's turret, and the panelled chamber where Sir Roger fought the duel with the Spanish cavalier, and the bedroom where Queen Elizabeth slept, and the banqueting-hall and the chapel where the Templar's heart is buried under the altar, and the gallery where Lady Euphrasia danced with King Henry VIII, in masquing dress, and the whispering corridor, and the painted room—"

"And the ghost-chamber, my lady? Oddly enough, that's the first room that American ladies ask to see! . . . But maybe your ladyship doesn't believe in ghosts, or the fact of its being late and getting dark."

Lady Wroth laughed quietly and sweetly. "Do you believe that the spirits of those who have passed on can only appear in the dark, dear Mrs. Ansdey?"

The housekeeper rustled her stiff silken skirts as she followed her new mistress up the broad staircase with its carven balusters and mossy carpets.

"I don't believe in ghosts at all, my lady!"

"Not in ghosts as they are commonly imagined; those shadowy white things that point and scare and hover," came floating back in the thin, sweet tones; "but in the spirits of the departed—it may be long-dead, or newly called from earth—who borrow for a little while the semblance in which they lived and loved, and return for one last look at a beloved home, or come for one dear glimpse of what might, but for the Infinite Eternal Will, have been a home. You believe in them, do you not? Or, if you do not now, you will! Ah, yes! you will, dear Mrs. Ansdey!"

Looking upwards from the hall, the butler saw the slight figure of Sir Vivian's bride traverse the first landing and pass out of view, followed by the portly figure of the housekeeper; and in that moment came the grind of wheels upon the avenue, a loud knock at the hall-door, and a sharp peal at the bell. Two liveried servants appearing in haste, admitted the master of the house, and at the first glimpse of Sir Vivian's ghastly face and torn and disordered garments, Cradell cried out in alarm.

"Sir Vivian—sir! It's worse than what my lady said! . . . You've been hurt! Shall I send for the doctor?"

"He is with us!" came the hoarse reply, and Cradell, peering out into the chill, gathering darkness, saw a strange carriage drawn up before the door, whose lamps threw a yellow reflection on the clouds of steam rising from the flanks of a pair of jaded horses. They were busy about the door; something was being lifted out? *What?* asked the old servant's shaking lips dumbly.

"Drove in from Greystoke . . . hospital carriage . . . Send the men to help . . . Get me some brandy," came

12

from Sir Vivian in hoarse shaking tones. "I can't . . . my arm . . . dislocated, that's all. I wish to Heaven—" His face expressed the nature of the wish, and the old butler cried with spirit, as he brought the brandy from the dining-room, "You should be thankful, sir, that you've been spared to her!"

"Spared to—her?"

The decanter clinked against the glass. Sir Vivian set it down upon the tray, and turned a white, seamed face and haggard eyes upon Cradell.

"Spared to my lady, sir, God bless her!" the old servant said. "Your hand shakes sadly; let me pour the brandy out."

Sir Vivian laughed, or made a grimace of laughter, showing his teeth and stretching his pale lips.

"Lord, sir! don't look like that!" Cradell begged. "Think if her ladyship were to see you! She—"

"If her ladyship were to see me!" repeated Sir Vivian. He drank off a glass of brandy and laughed again. "Cradell—are you mad, or am I?"

"Neither of us, sir, I hope!" said Cradell. Then a light broke upon him, and he cried, "Good gracious, Sir Vivian, is it possible that you don't know . . . my lady is here?"

"I know it." An awful agony was expressed in Sir Vivian's face. "I know it too well!" Great drops stood upon his forehead; he turned aside, clenching his hand, and fighting for self-command.

"She came half an hour ago," began the butler. "Me and Mrs. Ansdey were quite took aback. Mrs. Ansdey is upstairs with her ladyship now. . ."

"Man—man!" cried Sir Vivian, "do you know what you are saying?" He turned his streaming face upon the frightened butler and gripped him by the arm, fiercely . . .

"Lady Wroth—my wife, she is dead! There was an accident—she was killed instantaneously, with little pain,

13

thank God! They said so at the Greystoke Hospital . . . She is outside—there!" He pointed a shaking hand towards the partly open hall-door, through which a pale line of moonlight came stealing as the careful, measured tread of men carrying a precious burden sounded on the stone. "Yet you say to me—she arrived half an hour ago! You are raving—or I am delirious!"

For answer the butler pointed to the velvet mantle trimmed with costly sables that lay upon the floor.

"It's heaven's truth, Sir Vivian! And there lies the proof! . . . and here is Mrs. Ansdey to confirm it."

Both men looked up as the portly figure in its rustling black silken robes hurried down the great staircase.

"Sir Vivian! Oh, welcome home, Sir Vivian, a thousand times!" The housekeeper's face was very pale, her hands worked nervously, crumpling her fine lace apron. "But something dreadful has happened! it's written in your face!" she cried, "and God forgive a sinful woman, but I am beginning to believe that I have spoken with a spirit!"

"Cradell tells me that—" Sir Vivian made an upward gesture.

"It's true," cried Mrs. Ansdey. "Her ladyship—if 'twas her ladyship—explained that you were delayed. Someone was killed in the railway accident—"

"Someone was killed!"

"And you were coming on after you had seen to the wounded . . . She—she would not eat, or drink, or rest; she wished—all she wished was to see the house, and I obeyed, and we went through room after room until—there was a ring at the hall-door bell, and a knocking, and I turned to speak to my lady as we stood together in the painted chamber—and she was gone! Oh, Sir Vivian, what does it all mean?" cried Mrs. Ansdey.

"It means—this! . . . "

As the hall-door opened to admit the bearers with their precious burden, and as the men laid that cold, lovely, smiling image of Death reverently on the settle, the bloodhound wakened from his slumber and rising, uttered a long plaintive howl.

"Welcome home, my wife!" said Sir Vivian. "Now please to leave us here together!"

So the servants and the bearers withdrew.

"It was the same face!" Mrs. Ansdey whispered, as her faithful old comrade led her away. "Why did she come?"

Cradell said: "Because she'd made up her mind to—and she was a woman! There's two answers in one!"

He stooped mechanically to pick up the sable-trimmed mantle that had lain upon the floor. No hand had touched it, but it was no longer there.

A Spirit Elopement

When I exchanged my maiden name for better or worse, and dearest Vavasour and I, at the conclusion of the speeches—I was married in a travelling-dress of Bluefern's—descended the steps of mamma's house in Ebury Street—the Belgravian, *not* the Pimlican end—and, amid a hurricane of farewells and a hailstorm of pink and yellow and white *confetti*, stepped into the brougham that was to convey us to Waterloo Station, *en route* for Southampton—our honeymoon was to be spent in Guernsey—we were perfectly well satisfied with ourselves and each other. This state of mind is not uncommon at the outset of wedded life. You may have heard the horrid story of the newly-wedded cannibal chief, who remarked that he had never yet known a young bride to disagree with her husband in the early stages of the honeymoon. I believe if dearest Vavasour had seriously proposed to chop me into *cotêlettes* and eat me, with or without sauce, I should have taken it for granted that the powers that be had destined me to the high end of supplying one of the noblest of created beings with an *entrée* dish.

We were idiotically blissful for two or three days. It was flowery April, and Guernsey was looking her loveliest. No horrid hotel or boarding-house sheltered our lawful endearments. Some old friends of papa's had lent us an ancient mansion standing in a wild garden, now one pink riot of almond-blossom, screened behind lofty walls of lichened red brick and weather-worn, wrought-iron gates, painted yellow-white like all the other iron and wood work about the house.

"Mon Désir" the place was called, and the fragrance of potpourri yet hung about the old panelled salons. Vavasour wrote a sonnet—I have omitted to speak before of my husband's poetic gifts—all about the breath of new Passion stirring the fragrant dust of dead old Love, and the kisses of lips long mouldered that mingled with ours. It was a lovely sonnet, but crawly, as the poetical compositions of the Modern School are apt to be. And Vavasour was an enthusiastic convert to, and follower of, the Modern School. He had often told me that, had not his father heartlessly thrown him into his brewery business at the outset of his career—Sim's Mild and Bitter Ales being the foundation upon which the family fortunes were originally reared—he, Vavasour, would have been, ere the time of speaking, known to Fame, not only as a Minor Poet, but a Minor Decadent Poet—which trisyllabic addition, I believe, makes as advantageous a difference as the word "native" when attached to an oyster, or the guarantee "new laid" when employed with reference to an egg.

Dear Vavasour's temperament and tastes having a decided bias towards the gloomy and mystic, he had, before his great discovery of his latent poetical gifts, and in the intervals of freedom from the brain-carking and soul-stultifying cares of business, made several excursions into the regions of the Unknown. He had had some sort of intercourse with the Swedenborgians, and had mingled with the Muggletonians; he had coquetted with the Christian Scientists, and had been, until Theosophic Buddhism opened a wider field to his researches, an enthusiastic Spiritualist. But our engagement somewhat cooled his passion for psychic research, and when questioned by me with regard to table-rappings, manifestations, and materialisations, I could not but be conscious of a reticence in his manner of responding to my innocent desire for information. The reflection that he probably, like Canning's knife-grinder, had no story to tell, soon induced me to abandon the subject. I myself am somewhat reserved at this day in my method of dealing with the subject of spooks. But my silence does not proceed from ignorance.

Knowledge came to me after this fashion. Though the April sun shone bright and warm upon Guernsey, the island nights were chill. Waking by dear Vavasour's side—the novelty of this experience has since been blunted by the usage of years—somewhere between one and two o'clock towards break of the fourth day following our marriage, it occurred to me that a faint cold draught, with a suggestion of dampness about it, was blowing against my right cheek. One of the windows upon that side—our room possessed a rather unbecoming cross-light—had probably been left open. Dear Vavasour, who occupied the right side of our couch, would wake with toothache in the morning, or, perhaps, with mumps! Shuddering, as much at the latter idea as with cold, I opened my eyes, and sat up in bed with a definite intention of getting out of it and shutting the offending casement. Then I saw Katie for the first time.

She was sitting on the right side of the bed, close to dear Vavasour's pillow; in fact, almost hanging over it. From the first moment I knew that which I looked upon to be no creature of flesh and blood, but the mere apparition of a woman. It was not only that her face, which struck me as both pert and plain; her hands; her hair, which she wore dressed in an old-fashioned ringletty mode—in fact, her whole personality was faintly luminous, and surrounded by a halo of bluish phosphorescent light. It was not only that she was transparent, so that I saw the pattern of the old-fashioned, striped, dimity bed-curtain, in the shelter of which she sat, quite plainly through her. The consciousness was further conveyed to me by a voice—or the toneless, flat, faded impression of a voice—speaking faintly and clearly, not at my outer, but at my inner ear.

"Lie down again, and don't fuss. It's only Katie!" she said.

"Only Katie!" I liked that!

"I dare say you don't," she said tartly, replying as she had spoken, and I wondered that a ghost should exhibit such want of breeding. "But you have got to put up with me!"

"How dare you intrude here—and at such an hour!" I exclaimed mentally, for there was no need to wake dear Vavasour by talking aloud when my thoughts were read at sight by the ghostly creature who sat so familiarly beside him.

"I knew your husband before you did," responded Katie, with a faint phosphorescent sneer. "We became acquainted at a *séance* in North-West London soon after his conversion to Spiritualism, and have seen a great deal of each other from time to time." She tossed her shadowy curls with a possessive air that annoyed me horribly. "He was constantly materialising me in order to ask questions about Shakespeare. It is a standing joke in our Spirit world that, from the best educated spook in our society down to the most illiterate astral that ever knocked out 'rapport' with one 'p', we are all expected to know whether Shakespeare wrote his own plays, or whether they were done by another person of the same name."

"And which way was it?" I asked, yielding to a momentary twinge of curiosity.

Katie laughed mockingly. "There you go!" she said, with silent contempt.

"I wish *you* would!" I snapped back mentally. "It seems to me that you manifest a great lack of refinement in coming here!"

"I cannot go until Vavasour has finished," said Katie pertly. "Don't you see that he has materialised me by dreaming about me? And as there exists *at present*"—she placed an annoying stress upon the last two words—"a strong sympathy between you, so it comes about that I, as your husband's spiritual affinity, am visible to your waking perceptions. All the rest of the time I am hovering about you, though unseen."

"I call it detestable!" I retorted indignantly. Then I gripped my sleeping husband by the shoulder. "Wake up! wake up!" I cried aloud, wrath lending power to my grasp and a penetrative quality to my voice. "Wake up and leave off dreaming! I cannot and will not endure the presence of this creature another moment!"

"*Whaa*—" muttered my husband, with the almost inebriate incoherency of slumber, "*whasamaramydarling?*"

"Stop dreaming about that creature," I cried, "or I shall go home to Mamma!"

"Creature?" my husband echoed, and as he sat up I had the satisfaction of seeing Katie's misty, luminous form fade slowly into nothingness.

"You know who I mean!" I sobbed. "Katie—your spiritual affinity, as she calls herself!"

"You don't mean," shouted Vavasour, now thoroughly roused, "that you have *seen* her?"

"I do mean it," I mourned. "Oh, if I had only known of your having an entanglement with any creature of the kind, I would never have married you—never!"

"Hang her!" burst out Vavasour. Then he controlled himself, and said soothingly: "After all, dearest, there is nothing to be jealous of—"

"I jealous! And of that—" I was beginning, but Vavasour went on:

"After all, she is only a disembodied astral entity with whom I became acquainted—through my fifth principle, which is usually well developed—in the days when I moved in Spiritualistic society. She was, when living—for she died long before I was born—a young lady of very good family. I believe her father was a clergyman . . . and I will not deny that I encouraged her visits."

"Discourage them from this day!" I said firmly. "Neither think of her nor dream of her again, or I will have a separation."

"I will keep her, as much as possible, out of my waking thoughts," said poor Vavasour, trying to soothe me; "but a man cannot control his dreams, and she pervades mine in a manner which, even before our engagement, my pet, I began to find annoying. However, if she really is, as she has told me, a lady by birth and breeding, she will understand"—he raised his voice as though she were there and he intended her to hear—"that I am now a married man, and from this moment desire to have no further communication with her. Any suitable provision it is in my power to make—"

He ceased, probably feeling the difficulty he would have in explaining the matter to his lawyers; and it seemed to me that a faint mocking sniggle, or rather the auricular impression of it, echoed his words. Then, after some more desultory conversation, we fell soundly asleep. An hour may have passed when the same chilly sensation as of a damp draught blowing across the bed roused me. I rubbed my cheek and opened my eyes. They met the pale, impertinent smile of the hateful Katie, who was installed in her old post beside Vavasour's end of the bolster.

"You see," she said, in the same soundless way, and with a knowing little nod of triumph, "it is no use. He is dreaming of me again!"

21

"Wake up!" I screamed, snatching the pillow from under my husband's head and madly hurling it at the shameless intruder. This time Vavasour was almost snappish at being disturbed. Daylight surprised us in the middle of our first connubial quarrel. The following night brought a repetition of the whole thing, and so on, *da capo*, until it became plain to us, to our mutual disgust, that the more Vavasour strove to banish Katie from his dreams, the more persistently she cropped up in them. She was the most ill-bred and obstinate of astrals—Vavasour and I the most miserable of newly-married people. A dozen times in a night I would be roused by that cold draught upon my cheek, would open my eyes and see that pale, phosphorescent outline perched by Vavasour's pillow—nine times out of the dozen would be driven to frenzy by the possessive air and cynical smile of the spook. And although Vavasour's former regard for her was now converted into hatred, he found the thought of her continually invading his waking mind at the most unwelcome seasons. She had begun to appear to both of us *by day as well as by night* when our poisoned honeymoon came to an end, and we returned to town to occupy the house which Vavasour had taken and furnished in Sloane Street. I need only mention that Katie accompanied us.

Insufficient sleep and mental worry had by this time thoroughly soured my temper no less than Vavasour's. When I charged him with secretly encouraging the presence I had learned to hate, he rudely told me to think as I liked! He implored my pardon for this brutality afterwards upon his knees, and with the passage of time I learned to endure the presence of his attendant shade with patience. When she nocturnally hovered by the side of my sleeping spouse, or in constituence no less filmy than a whiff of cigarette-smoke, appeared at his elbow in the face of day, I saw her plainly, and at these moments she would favour me with a significant contraction of the eyelid, which was, to say the least of it, unbecoming in a spirit who had been a clergyman's daughter. After one of these experiences it was that the idea which I afterwards carried into execution occurred to me.

I began by taking in a few numbers of a psychological publication entitled *The Spirit-Lamp*. Then I formed the acquaintance of Madame Blavant, the renowned Professoress of Spiritualism and Theosophy. Everybody has heard of Madame, many people have read her works, some have heard her lecture. I had heard her lecture. She was a lady with a strong determined voice and strong determined features. She wore her plentiful grey hair piled in sibylline coils on the top of her head, and—when she lectured—appeared in a white Oriental silk robe that fell around her tall gaunt figure in imposing folds. This robe was replaced by one of black satin when she held her *séances*. At other times, in the seclusion of her study, she was draped in an ample gown of Indian chintz innocent of cut, but yet imposing. She smiled upon my new-born desire for psychic instruction, and when I had subscribed for a course of ten private *séances* at so many guineas a piece she smiled more.

Madame lived in a furtive, retiring house, situated behind high walls in Endor's Grove, N.W. A long glass tunnel led from the garden gate to the street door, for the convenience of Mahatmas and other persons who preferred privacy. I was one of those persons, for not for spirit worlds would I have had Vavasour know of my repeated visits to Endor's Grove. Before these were over I had grown quite indifferent to supernatural manifestations, banjos and accordions that were thrummed by invisible performers, blood-red writing on mediums' wrists, mysterious characters in slate-pencil, Planchette, and the Table Alphabet. And I had made and improved upon acquaintance with Simon.

Simon was a spirit who found me attractive. He tried in his way to make himself agreeable, and, with my secret motive in view—let me admit without a blush—I encouraged him. When I knew I had him thoroughly in hand, I attended no more *séances* at Endor's Grove. My purpose was accomplished upon a certain night, when, feeling my shoulder violently shaken, I opened the eyes which had been closed in simulated slumber to meet the indignant glare of my husband. I glanced over his shoulder. Katie did not occupy her usual place. I turned my glance towards the arm-chair which stood at my side of the bed. It was not vacant. As I guessed, it was occupied by Simon. There he sat, the luminously transparent appearance of a weak-chinned, mild-looking young clergyman, dressed in the obsolete costume of eighty years previously. He gave me a bow in which respect mingled with some degree of complacency, and glanced at Vavasour.

"I have been explaining matters to your husband," he said, in that soundless spirit-voice with which Katie had first made me acquainted. "He understands that I am a clergyman and a reputable spirit, drawn into your life-orbit by the irresistible attraction which your mediumistic organisation exercises over my—"

"There, you hear what he says!" I interrupted, nodding confirmatively at Vavasour. "Do let me go to sleep!"

"What, with that intrusive beast sitting beside you?" shouted Vavasour indignantly. "Never!"

"Think how many months I have put up with the presence of Katie!" said I. "After all, it's only tit for tat!" And the ghost of a twinkle in Simon's pale eye seemed to convey that he enjoyed the retort.

Vavasour grunted sulkily, and resumed his recumbent position. But several times that night he awakened me with renewed objurgations of Simon, who with unflinching resolution maintained his post. Later on I started from sleep to find Katie's usual seat occupied. She looked less pert and confident than usual, I thought, and rather humbled and fagged, as though she had had some trouble in squeezing her way into Vavasour's sleeping thoughts. By day, after that night, she seldom appeared. My husband's brain was too much occupied with Simon, who assiduously haunted me. And it was now my turn to twit Vavasour with unreasonable jealousy. Yet though I gloried in the success of my stratagem, the continual presence of that couple of spooks was an unremitting strain upon my nerves.

But at length an extraordinary conviction dawned on my mind, and became stronger with each successive night. Between Simon and Katie an acquaintance had sprung up. I would awaken, or Vavasour would arouse, to find them gazing across the barrier of the bolster which divided them with their pale negatives of eyes, and chatting in still, spirit voices. Once I started from sleep to find myself enveloped in a kind of mosquito-tent of chilly, filmy vapour, and the conviction rushed upon me that He and She had leaned across our couch and exchanged an intangible embrace. Katie was the leading spirit in this, I feel convinced—there was no effrontery about Simon. Upon the next night I, waking, overheard a fragment of conversation between them which plainly revealed how matters stood.

"We should never have met upon the same plane," remarked Simon silently, "but for the mediumistic intervention of these people. Of the man"—he glanced slightingly towards Vavasour—"I cannot truthfully say I think much. The lady"—he bowed in my direction—"is everything that a lady should be!"

"You are infatuated with her, it is plain!" snapped Katie, "and the sooner you are removed from her sphere of influence the better."

"Her power with me is weakening," said Simon, "as Vavasour's is with you. Our outlines are no longer so clear as they used to be, which proves that our astral individualities are less strongly impressed upon the brains of our earthly sponsors than they were. We are still materialised; but how long this will continue——" He sighed and shrugged his shoulders.

"Don't let us wait for a formal dismissal, then," said Katie boldly. "Let us throw up our respective situations."

"I remember enough of the Marriage Service to make our union, if not regular, at least respectable," said Simon.

"And I know quite a fashionable place on the Outside Edge of Things, where we could settle down," said Katie, "and live practically on nothing."

I blinked at that moment. When I saw the room again clearly, the chairs beside our respective pillows were empty.

Years have passed, and neither Vavasour nor myself has ever had a glimpse of the spirits whom we were the means of introducing to one another. We are quite content to know ourselves deprived for ever of their company. Yet sometimes, when I look at our three babies, I wonder whether that establishment of Simon's and Katie's on the Outside Edge of Things includes a nursery.

Lilium Peccatorum

I t arrived by itself in a neatly-labelled green-paper bag on the top of a five-guinea assortment of garden flower-bulbs packed in husks. Nobody was in a position to afford any information about the appearance of the thing when grown. The head-gardener consequently assumed an air of mystery masking an ignorance as profound as our own, potted the bulb in patent cocoanut-fibre, and put it in the greenhouse with the daffodils, on the shelf below the paper-white narcissus-polyanthus.

"*Lilium peccatorum*," said Didi, hanging over the pot containing the mystery (Didi is the wife of the head-gardener's employer). "What an odd name! Why do they stick long, solemn, crack-jaw Latin names on to the poor dear flowers? It must hurt them, I can't help feeling, when all they want is to grow up and be lovely and sweet. *Lilium peccatorum!*" She made a face.

"Perhaps it means the Sin Lily," suggested the employer of the head-gardener.

"What a funny yellow horn it has begun to send up!" gushed Didi. "I feel frightfully anxious to see it in blossom."

"Wait until April, then," said Didi's better-half.

"I don't feel as though I could; but, of course, I have got to," said Didi wistfully.

It did not seem as though her patience was going to be taxed so far. The *Lilium peccatorum* grew apace, and waxed greater every day. It had a devouring appetite for

27

liquid manure, and an insatiable ambition to grow taller and taller. In shape it resembled an arum lily, though it was three times as big, and when a long green stalk, with a paler green slipper at one end of it, rose from a fold of brown-grey stem-sheathing, Didi held her breath with anticipation.

"What colour is it going to be, I wonder?" Didi would say twenty times a week. "Not white, because I can see spots and streaks and dapples coming. Oh, how my head aches!"

"You have been spending too much time in the greenhouse," said the owner of it and of Didi, judicially. "I have told Welsh that, for a greenhouse, the temperature is abnormally high, and the coke-bill corresponds. But it is no use talking to that man."

"If you only *talked*, and didn't scold and swear," hinted Didi.

" 'Scold and swear'! . . . Is thy servant an Australian parrot that he should do these things?" said Didi's husband.

"You can turn it off with a joke if you like, but you never do come out of the greenhouse in a good temper," declared Didi, obstinately. "I don't believe it agrees with you."

"Possibly not," said Didi's owner. "And that brings us back to my original remark about the temperature of the—"

"Bother the temperature!" screamed Didi, her own shooting many degrees above boiling-point. And she violently hurled a yellow-ticketed Mudie novel to the other end of the sofa, where she had been sitting with one knee tucked under her—a favourite posture of Didi's—knitting a silk necktie in a conservative shade of blue for the man whom she had sworn to obey. The title of the missile was *The Mirage of Marriage*, by "One Who Has Parched by the Lake of Glittering Dust."

"Really, my dear Didi," her husband was beginning, when Peter and Paul, the fox-terriers, flew at Dandy, the Skye, and tried to divide him between them.

"Down, you brutes! Let go!" thundered Didi's proprietor, holding a string of dogs aloft by the simple process of lifting Peter by the tail, who had his teeth fixed in Dandy's hairy scruff, who held Paul firmly gripped by the loose skin of the shoulder. "One would think they had been spending the morning in the greenhouse too," he remarked, with more point than delicacy, "they are so confoundedly quarrelsome."

"You know they follow me everywhere," said Didi, replacing her knitting in the basket, and sweeping out of the room.

The dogs swept out, too, meeting Timour, the Persian cat, on the threshold. A brief scuffle ensued, several resounding slaps were punctuated by as many shrill yelps, and Timour, swelled out to thrice his bulk, and with a tail like a Spanish broom-bush, rushed like a spitting projectile through the drawing-room, and vanished by an open window.

"I saw the cat watching a rat-hole in the greenhouse to-day," said Didi's voice from outside the window. "Probably your coke-bill has upset him." An acid little laugh followed. Then silence. And Prescott came in to say that the head-gardener would be glad of a moment of his employer's leisure. Two of the under-gardeners who had been busy all day carrying pots between the retarding house and the greenhouse, had exchanged words, finally blows. And the cook had expressed herself in such terms with regard to a consignment of seakale and parsnips for kitchen use that Mr. Welsh merely wished to drop the following sentence: "Either that spitfire goes, or I do!"

"What the deuce is the matter with everybody? Is there thunder in the air?" pondered the master of this disturbed household. "Where was the cook when she told you your vegetables were rubbish like yourself and your family? In the kitchen, cooking? Because the effect of a glowing 'Triplex' register, combined with anxiety as to—ah! flavouring and so forth . . . allowances must be made for—"

"Sir," said Mr. Welsh, "the outrage was offered on my own ground, so to speak. I refer to the large upper green'ouse, where we are usually busy at this time of year. To-morrow being Sunday, and the privilege customary in good houses, cook had looked in about a spray of Neapolitan violets to match a new bonnet—"

"Looked in! At the greenhouse? . . . Upon my soul! The devil must be in the place!" ejaculated its owner.

"Sir," said Mr. Welsh, "being a Cymric Free Methodist, I have no acquaintance with the personage named. By the way, it may interest you to know that the *Lilium peccatorum*, concerning which my lady has expressed a good deal of interest, is in the act of bloom."

"Is it? Very well. I'll go and have a look at it," said my lady's husband. He threw on a cap and stepped out at the glass door of his own pleasant den, into the spring sweetness of the garden. The crocus borders blazed yellow in the afternoon sun, the hepatica and the scillas starred the gold bands with amethyst and turquoise. The thrushes sang, and the black sand of the well-kept paths crunched under his feet with a crisp, pleasant sound. And so to the upper greenhouse, where a surprise awaited him. The great green slipper bud of the *Lilium peccatorum* had bleached to cream outside, and the great single petal had opened in a magnificent aspiring whorl, showing the interior, darkly red as rich blood, and dappled with orange, white, and black. A black, shining, snake-like pistil rose from the ovary, towering a foot and higher above the volute, and round the marvellous flower buzzed a distracted bevy of flies, drunken with the intolerable odour, as of carrion, which the lily exhaled.

The owner of the flower, breathing it, sickened. He drew his handkerchief from his pocket, and, covering his mouth and nose, drew near the intolerable splendour. The crown of the pistil he saw, as he craned further, ended in an orifice through which fly after fly crawled and disappeared. None of the eager trespassers ever came back, and the carrion odour grew stronger as the newly-opened flower devoured its first living meal.

That intolerable odour, how it first sickened, then stimulated the sense! How the brain responded and the throbbing heart sent forth gushes of thick red blood into the pulsating arteries, only to receive it back, purified by the narrow channels of the veins! What a mystery Life was! What a still greater mystery, Love! Love for a woman, evil, tigerish, and lovely as the Lily of Sin itself, incarnate passion answering to the primal desire, richest fuel for the most devouring flame. Only one woman like *that* in the world. And Didi's husband had left her for Didi. Why not go back? Take up the crimson thread where it had been dropped and weave it with the web of Life again . . . Why not?

He asked himself the question with an intolerable yearning, an irresistible longing to be free, to go back. The hand that had stretched out of the Past to grip his heart and squeeze out the wine of memory from its veins, kept hold; its white fellow beckoned. He felt her breath on him, he saw her eyes, and as he gasped for breath the carrion odour of the Sin Lily seemed changed to indescribable sweetness.

He reeled away from it with his hand before his eyes, with the settled determination that, in spite of oaths made before heaven and to a woman who counted nothing now, he would go back to that other without delay. He could get to Victoria Station in time for the last Dover Express, he could cross by the night boat, be in Paris by five o'clock, next morning. He could tell his man to pack his bag, he would wire from Paris to his solicitors. Didi should have her way made plain for the—for the divorce.

And then he heard her voice and another's at the greenhouse door. He drew back instinctively under a high shelf, and a dainty, pink-blossomed, luxuriantly-growing begonia drooping from above made a screen before him. He heard Didi's trilling, silvery little laugh, a manly guffaw responded, and the reflection of a cavalry moustache was caught in a pane of the opening door as it swung back against the drooping pink trails of the begonia.

"Oh—h! what an awful smell!" shrieked Didi.

"Where does it come from?" asked the cavalry moustache. It belonged to a previously-rejected suitor of Didi's, who owned a country place and had motored over to call. "Has the gardener been usin' 'Rough on Rats'? Ought to try the new virus. Never have myself, but they say—"

Didi did not hear; her handkerchief was over her little nose. She fixed her eyes admiringly upon the panther-like, evil beauty of the Sin Lily, and gasped, partly from admiration of the flower, partly in disgust at its odour. "Isd't the thig spleddid?" she asked, through the handkerchief. "Rodald bought it with sobe Dutch bulbs—ad dobody kdows adythig about it. Do look ad the flies, buzzing about it—poor things!—ad gettig eaten up."

The face that wore the cavalry moustache had become livid, the brown eyes burned with a sombre red light. "Just as men buzz about some women and get swallowed before the eyes of the others who're waiting to come on. Do you know, Didi . . . I may call you Didi still, I suppose?"

"Goodness, why not?" asked Didi, removing the handkerchief.

"Do you know, I've seen a woman exactly like that big red lily. Quite as fascinating, quite as poisonous. I'm ready to bet the thing's poisonous, though I don't know, you know. Saw her in Paris, three or four years ago, and had just strength of mind to run for my life."

"Why?" lisped Didi. Her blue eyes shone like sapphires, and her cheeks were stained geranium red. Her black hair clung in silky tendrils to the delicate temples; there was a silver comb of Spanish work in the topmost coil, with dull uncut rubies winking in it. And she wore a creamy-hued gown of clinging cashmere under her sable cloak. "Why did you run for your life?"

"Because I had the courage to act like an honourable man," came the rough answer. Then: "I haven't the courage now!" cried Didi's old lover, and seized her hands, in a strenuous, eager grip, and kissed them with hot devouring lips. "Oh! Didi! I love you, ten thousand times more idiotically than ever!" he cried. "Are you going to play the married prude, and tell me to go away?"

"No!" said Didi, and the word fell like a hammer-stroke on the heart of the listener, who had, you will remember, so fully made up his mind to cross over to Paris by the night's mail. Something whizzed in his right temple, like a clock running down. He moved slightly, in his pink-blossomed, perfumed hiding-place, and shut his eyes to hide what he feared to see.

When he opened them Didi was gone. The other man stood looking at the Sin Lily with bloodshot eyes. And the carrion odour was no longer perceptible, and whiffs of heavy, silencing sweetness came to the nostrils of Didi's husband and Didi's lover.

"I'm a d——d blackguard, I suppose, but I mean to go on being one," said the man with the cavalry moustache. "My cosmos is all *Ego—et Illa*. And I'll take her away, whenever

33

I can get her to go, and face the music, though," an ugly smile curved the heavy moustache, "there's an old proverb about stolen kisses . . . Gad! how sweet that crimson lily smells. And I thought it stank like troops' quarters on a South African transport with the ports all shut and the hatches battened down. Halloa! Somebody coming! She? How like a daughter of Eve! No! . . . they're servants. If they'd heard me talking out loud to myself like a man in a rotten play, they'd have said I was off my chump. Well, I *am*!"

The door opened and—

"Beg pardon, sir! No idea you were still here," said the voice of the head-gardener. "I thought I saw you leave with my lady a minute ago."

"Just going, thanks. Only stopped to look at the new lily," said the voice of Didi's old friend. And as his long legs carried him away and out of the story, the respectable Mr. Welsh ushered into the greenhouse Didi's maid.

"Don't mention it, Miss Todds," said the civil Mr. Welsh, "always glad to oblige any member of the house staff, as I hope you're aware. This is the new flower you're desirous of seeing, and if you don't object to the hodour, which is a bit off at the first whiff, a handsomer bloom you couldn't wish to see."

"My, but don't it smell chronic!" cried Todds, curiously sniffing the foetid exhalations of the magnificent flower.

"It is not so sweet as the breath of a Halderney cow, or of a pretty young woman, which is next best," said the respectable Mr. Welsh, drawing close to the undeniably attractive Todds.

"The idea! Puttin' the cow first—I do call that polite!" giggled Todds.

"There certainly are cows *and* cows," said Mr. Welsh, and surely his opaque little black eyes twinkled outrageously.

Surely his respectable tweed sleeve, with the darn that Mrs. Welsh had sat up late to fine-draw, had no right to encircle thus boldly the waist of my lady's maid. But Miss Todds was not angry. On the contrary, she giggled again.

"Naughty!" she said, with a provocative slap on the back of the intrusive hand.

"Miss Todds, I love you!" burst from the respectable Mr. Welsh.

"And you a married man!" gurgled Miss Todds, her curls and coils and waves infringing upon the married man's shoulder.

"Love laughs at laws," said Mr. Welsh, with great originality. "If you don't believe me—ask the cook. Married to a butler, in place not a mile away, old enough to know better, yet what do she do? Makes me a declaration of unbridled passion only this very morning in this very place—on pretence of seeing me about vegetables for the 'ouse, and if Mrs. Welsh knew, she'd have her eyes out."

"And suppose Mrs. Welsh saw you now?" was the pertinent question of the fair embraced. "What do you suppose she'd do to you?"

The reply of Mr. Welsh was a double-barrelled chirp.

"Lor! you bold-faced man, you!" exclaimed Miss Todds. "And you a stric' Methodist! I'm ashamed of you!"

In what terms the enamoured head-gardener would have replied can only be conjectured, as his employer at the psychological moment stepped from behind the screen of the begonia. Miss Todds shrieked and vanished. Welsh, petrified by sudden consternation into the mere image of a head-gardener in the act of touching his cap, remained awaiting judgment.

"And what are you going to say for yourself? It strikes me that you will have some trouble to explain what I have seen just now?" demanded his employer cruelly.

"Sir," began Mr. Welsh, "we are all mortal, frail beings, and equally liable to be overtook by temptation. And"—he wiped his forehead—"temptation seems to be in the air just now."

"Just so. Take up that pot there, with the *Lilium peccatorum* in it; carry it to the forcing-house stoking-pit and burn it in the furnace—bulb and all. And if I should call you back and tell you not to carry out the order"—the speaker bit his lips and clenched his hands as though the words cost an effort—"don't obey me. Do you hear?"

"I do, sir," said the relieved Mr. Welsh. He took up the Sin Lily and went out, the scarlet, black, and tawny banner of the uncanny flower flaunting high above the level of his head.

"The thing is done?" asked he who had commanded it a few moments later. "You have burned the lily—every scrap of it?"

"Every bit, sir," said Mr. Welsh, whose look was still dazed. "And if you'll believe me, in the final shrivel, if I may so put it, the flower give a groan."

"Go home to your wife," said Didi's husband, "and don't let what I saw just now occur again."

"It shall not, sir," said Mr. Welsh positively. "The irregularity must have been the outcome of a momentary rush of blood to the brain. Looking back upon it with a calmer mind, I can't comprehend how it happened."

"I can," muttered his employer, "or that *Lilium peccatorum* has been named for nothing. Phew! what an escape!"

With his own brain now cool and his own impulses in a strictly regulated condition, he passed on to the house. The gardeners who had quarrelled in the morning were peaceably exchanging tobacco-boxes. Didi and the dogs met him a little farther on. All four looked humble and apologetic.

36

"Has Emiston gone?" asked Didi's husband, referring to the owner of the cavalry moustache.

"At least an hour ago," said Didi, shrugging her slim shoulders. Wheels were heard on the drive, and directly afterwards a servant brought Didi a note written in haste by the owner of the cavalry moustache, and sent over per dog-cart and groom.

"Forgive me for being such an idiot. Can't imagine how I came to forget myself so thoroughly. Am leaving for Paris to-night. —E." she read aloud.

"So he made an idiot of himself, did he?" asked Didi's better-half.

"In the greenhouse," admitted Didi, "and I told him 'No!' he needn't go away, but I suppose he thinks it's best. By-and-by he will come back and be sensible and marry Vicky Newingly."

"If I had gone away, as I fully meant to do, while the spell of that infernal flower was upon me, should *I* have come back and been sensible?" pondered Didi's husband. And he did not ponder aloud—and it was just as well.

A Vanished Hand

"Why," Daymond wrote, "*do you imagine that I shall despise you for this confession? None but a whole-souled, high-hearted woman could have made it! You have said you love me, frankly; and I say in return that had the fountains of my heart not been hopelessly dried up at their sources, they must have sprung forth gladly at such words from you. But the passion of love, dear friend, it is for me no more to know; and I hold you in too warm regard to offer you, in exchange for shekels of pure Ophir gold, a defaced and worthless coinage!*"

As Daymond penned the closing words of the sentence, the last rays of the smoky-red London sunset were withdrawn. Only a little while ago he had replenished the fire with fresh logs; but they were damp, and charred slowly, giving forth no pleasant flame. He struck a match and lighted a taper that stood upon his writing table. It created a feeble oasis of yellow radiance upon the darkness of the great studio, and the shadow of Daymond's head and shoulders bending above it, was cast upward in gigantesque caricature upon the skylight, reduced to frosty white opacity by a burden of March snow.

Daymond poised the drying pen in white, well-kept fingers, and read over what he had written. Underlying all the elegance of well-modelled phrases was the sheer brutality of rejection, definitely expressed. His finely strung mental organisation revolted painfully at the imperative necessity of being cruel.

"She asks for bread," he cried aloud, "and I am giving her a stone!" The lofty walls and domed roof of his workshop gave back the words to him, and his sensitive ear noted the theatrical twang of the echo. Yet the pang of remorse that had moved him to speech was quite genuine.

"You have heard my story," he wrote on.

A great many people had heard it, and had been bored by it; but, sensitive as Daymond's perceptions were, he was not alive to this fact.

"Seventeen years ago, while I was still a student dreaming of fame in a draughty Paris studio, I met the woman who was destined—I felt it then as I know it now—to be the one love of my life. She was an American, a little older than myself. She was divinely beautiful to me—I hardly know whether she was really so or not. We gave up all, each for each. She left husband, home, friends, to devote her life to me. I—"

He paused, trying to sum up the list of his own sacrifices, and ultimately left the break, as potent to express much, and went on:

"Guilty as I suppose we were, we were happy together—how happy I dare not even recall. Twenty-four months our life together lasted, and then came the end. It was the cholera year in Paris; the year which brought me my first foretaste of success in Art, robbed me of all joy in life . . . She died. Horribly! suddenly! And the best of me lies buried in her grave!"

The muscles of his throat tightened with the rigor that accompanies emotion; his eyelids smarted. He threw back his still handsome head, and a tear fell shining on the delicately scented paper underneath his hand. He looked at the drop as it spread and soaked into a damp little circle, and made no use of the blotting paper to remove the stain. If any crudely candid observer had told Daymond that he dandled this desolation of his—took an aesthetic delight in his devotion to the coffined handful of dust that had once lived and palpitated at his touch, he would have been honestly outraged and surprised. Yet the thing was true. He had made his sorrow into a hobby-horse during the last fifteen years of honest regret, of absolute faithfulness to the memory of his dead mistress. It gratified him to see the well-trained creature dance and perform the tricks of the *haute école*. He was aware that the romance of that past, which he regretted with such real sincerity, added something to the glamour of his achieved reputation, his established fame, in the eyes of the world. The halo which it cast about him had increased his desirability in the eyes of the great lady who, after affording him numberless unutilised opportunities for the declaration of a sentiment which her large handsome person and her large handsome property had inspired in many other men, had written him a frank, womanly letter, placing these unreservedly at his disposal . . . And Daymond, in his conscious fidelity and unconscious vanity, must perforce reply wintrily, nipping with the east wind of non-reciprocity the mature passion-tendrils which sought to twine themselves about him. It was a painful task, though the obligation of it tickled him agreeably—another proof of the inconsistency of the man, who may be regarded as a type of humanity; for we are all veritable Daymonds, in that the medium which gives us back to our own gloating eyes day by day is never the crystal mirror of Truth, but such a lying glass as the charlatans of centuries agone were wont to make for ancient Kings and withered Queens to mop and mow in.

Daymond pushed back his chair, and got up, and began to pace from end to end of the studio. The costly Moorish carpets muffled the falling of his footsteps, which intermittently sounded on the polished interspaces of the parqueted floor, and then were lost again in velvet silence. In the same way, his tall figure, with its thoughtfully bending head and hands clasped behind it, would be swallowed up among the looming shadows of tall easels or faintly glimmering suggestions of sculptured figures which here and there thrust portions of limbs, or angles of faces, out of the dusk—to appear again with the twilit north window for its background, or emerge once more upon the borders of the little island of taper-shine. So he moved amid the works of his genius restlessly and wearily to and fro; and the incoherent mutterings which broke from him showed that his thoughts were running, in the beaten track of years.

"If I could see her again—if our eyes and lips and hands and hearts might meet for even the fraction of a minute, as they used to do, it would be enough. I could wait then patiently through the slow decay of the cycles for the turning of the key in the rusty wards, and the clanking of my broken fetters on the echoing stone, and the burst of light that shall herald my deliverance from prison! . . . " He lifted his arms above his head. "Oh, my dead love, my dear love! if you are near, as I have sometimes fancied you were, speak to me, touch me—once, only once! . . . " He waited a moment with closed eyelids and outstretched hands, and then, with a dry sob of baffled longing, stumbled back to his writing table, where the little taper was flickering its last, and dropped into his arm-chair.

"And other women talk of love to me. What wonder I am cold as ice to them, remembering her!"

It was a scene he had gone through scores upon scores of times—words and gestures varying according to the pathetic inspiration of the moment. He knew that he was pale, and that his eyes were bleared with weeping, and he had a kind of triumph in the knowledge that the pain

41

of retrospective longing and of present loneliness was so poignantly real and keen. Out of the blackness behind his chair at that moment came a slight stir and rustle—not the sough of a vagrant draught stirring among folds of tapestry, but an undeniably human sound. But half-displeased with the suspicion that there had been a witness to his agony, he turned—turned and saw Her, the well-beloved of the old, old time, standing very near him.

Beyond a vivid sensation of astonishment, he felt little. He did not tremble with fear—what was there in that perfectly familiar face to fear? He did not fall, stammering with incoherent rapture, at her feet. And yet, a few moments ago, he had felt that for one such sight of her, returned from the Unknowable to comfort him—dragged back from the mysterious Beyond by his strong yearnings—he would have bartered fame, honour, and wealth—submitted his body to unheard-of tortures—shed his blood to the last heart's drop. He had prayed that a miracle might be performed—and the prayer had been granted. He had longed—desperately longed—to look on her once more—and the longing was satisfied. And he could only stare wide-eyed, and gape with dropped jaw, and say stupidly:

"*You?*"

For answer she turned her face—in hue, and line, and feature, no one whit altered—so that the light might illumine it fully, and stood so regarding him in silence. Every pore of her seemed to drink in the sight of him;— her lips were parted in breathless expectancy. Every hair of the dark head—dressed in the fashion of fifteen years ago; every fold of the loose dress she wore—a garment he knew again; every lift and fall of her bosom seemed to cry out dumbly to him. There was a half-quenched spark glimmering in each of her deep eyes, that might have wanted only one breath from his mouth to break out into flame. Her hands hung clasped before her. It seemed as if they were only waiting for the signal to unclasp—for the outspread arms to summon him to her heart again. But the signal did not come. He caught a breath, and repeated, dully:

"You! It is you?"

She returned:

"It is I!"

The well-known tones! Recollection upsprang in his heart like a gush of icy waters. For a moment he was thrilled to the centre of his being. But the smitten nerve chords ceased to vibrate in another moment, and he rose to offer her a chair.

She moved across and took it, as he placed it by the angle of the wide hearth; and lifted her skirts aside with a movement that came back to him from a long way off, like her tone in speaking—and, shading her deep grey eyes from the dull red heat with her white left hand, looked at him intently. He, having pushed his own seat back into the borders of the shadowland beyond the taper's gleam and the hearth glow, looked back at her. That hand of hers bore no ring. When he had broken the plain gold link that had fettered it in time past, he had set in its place a ruby that had belonged to his mother. The ruby was on his finger now. He hid it out of sight in the pocket of his velvet painting coat, not knowing why he did so. And at that moment she broke the silence with:

"You see I have come to you at last!"

He replied, with conscious heaviness:

"Yes—I see!"

"Has the time seemed long? . . . We have no time, you know, where . . . Is it many days since? . . . "

"Many days!"

"My poor Robert! . . . Weeks? . . . Months? . . . Not years? . . . "

"Fifteen years . . . "

"Fifteen years! And you have suffered all that time. Oh, cruel! cruel! If there was more light here, I might see your face more plainly. Dear face! I shall not love it less if there are lines and marks of grief upon it—it will not seem less handsome to me at forty than it did at twenty-five! Ah, I wish there was more light!" The old pettishly coaxing tones! "But yet I do not wish for it, lest it should show you any change in *me*!"

"You are not changed in the least." He drew breath hard. "It might be yesterday—," he said, and left the sentence unfinished.

"I am glad," said the voice that he had been wont to recall to memory as wooingly sweet. "They have been kinder than I knew . . . Oh! it has always been so painful to recall," she went on, with the old little half shrug, half shudder, "that I died an *ugly* death—that I was not pretty to look at as I lay in my coffin! . . . "

Daymond recoiled inwardly. That vanity, in a woman, should not be eradicated by the fact of her having simply ceased to exist, was an hypothesis never before administered for his mental digestion.

"How curiously it all happened," she said, her full tones trembling a little. "It was autumn—do you remember?— and the trees in the Bois and the gardens of the Luxembourg were getting yellowy brown. There were well-dressed crowds walking on the Boulevards, and sitting round the little tables outside the restaurants. One could smell chloride of lime and carbolic acid crossing the gutters, and see the braziers burning at the corners of infected streets, and long strings of hearses going by; but nothing seemed so unlikely as that either of us should be taken ill and die. We were too wicked, you said, and too happy! . . . only the good, miserable people were carried off, because any other world would be more suitable to them than this . . . It was nonsense, of course, but it served us to laugh at. Then, because you could not sell your great Salon picture, and we could not afford the expense, you gave a supper at the *Café des Trois Oiseaux* (*Cabinet particulier No. 6*)—and Valéry and the others joined us. I was so happy that night . . . my new dress became me . . . I wore yellow roses— your favourite Maréchal Niel's. When I was putting them in my bosom and my hair you came behind and kissed me on the shoulder. *O, mon Dieu! mon Dieu!* I can feel it now! We went to the Variétés, and then to supper. I had never felt so gay. People are like that, I remember having heard, just when they are going to die. Valéry gaped—I believe he was half in love with me—and I teased him because I knew you would be jealous. In those days you would have been jealous of the studio *écorché*. Ha! ha! ha!"

Daymond shuddered. The recurrent French phrases jarred on him; something in her voice and manner scarified inexpressibly his sensitive perceptions. He wondered, dumbly, whether she had always been like this? She went on:

"And then, suddenly, in the midst of the laughter, the champagne, the good dishes—the pains of hell!" She shuddered. "And then a blank, and waking up in bed at the hospital, still in those tortures—and getting worse and seeing in your white face that I was going to die! Drip-drip! I could feel your tears falling upon my face, upon my hand; but I was even impatient of you in my pain. Once I fancied that I heard myself saying that I hated you. Did I really?"

"I think—I believe you did! But, of course—" Daymond stopped, and shuddered to the marrow as she leaned across to him caressingly, so near that her draperies brushed his knee and her breath fanned upon his face.

45

"Imagine it!" she cried, "that I *hated* you! *You* to whom I had given myself—you for whom I left my—"

He interrupted, speaking in an odd, strained voice: "Never mind that now."

"I had always wished to die first," she resumed, "but not in that way; not without leaving you a legacy of kind words and kisses. Ah!" (her voice stole to his ears most pleadingly), "do you know that I have been here, I cannot tell how long, and you have not kissed me once, darling?"

She rose up in her place—she would have come to him, but he sprang to his feet, and thrust out both hands to keep her off, crying:

"No! no!"

She sank back into her seat, looking at him wide-eyed and wonderingly. "Is he afraid of me?" she whispered to herself.

"I am not afraid of you," Daymond returned almost roughly. "But you must make allowances for me at first. Your sudden coming—the surprise—"

"Ah yes! the surprise—and the joy—?"

He cleared his throat and looked another way. He was shamedly conscious that the emotion that stiffened his tongue and hampered his gestures was something widely different from joy. He spoke again, confusedly. "This seems like old times—before—"

"Before I died," she said, "without bidding good-bye to you. Dear! if you guessed how I have longed to know what you said and did when it was all over, you would not mind telling me . . . *'Are they grieving—those whom I have left behind?'* is a question that is often asked in the place I come from. You were sorry? You cried? Ah! I know you must have cried!"

"I believe," Daymond returned, moving restlessly in his chair, "that I did. And I—I kissed you, though the doctors

46

told me not to. I wanted to catch the cholera and die, too, I believe! . . . "

"Yes?"

"And when the people came with—the coffin, I"—he bit his lip—"I would not let them touch you! . . . "

"My poor boy!"

He winced from the tenderness. He felt with indescribable sensations the light pressure of that well-known once well-loved touch upon his arm.

"And then—after the funeral, I believe I had a brain fever." He passed his hand through his waving, slightly grizzled hair, as if to assist his lagging memory—really, as an excuse for shaking off that intolerable burden of her hand. "And when I recovered I found there was no way to forgetfulness"—he heard her sigh faintly—"except through work. I worked then—I am working still."

"Always alone?"

"Generally alone. I have never married."

"Of course not!"

A faint dissent began to stir in him at this matter-of-fact acquiescence in his widowed turtle-like celibacy. "It may interest you to know," he observed, with a touch of the pompous manner which had grown upon him with the growth of his reputation, "that my career has been successful in the strongest sense of the word. I became, I may say, one of the leaders of the world of Art. Upon the decease or resignation of the President of the ——, it is more than probable that I shall be invited to occupy his vacant place. And an intimation has reached me, from certain eminent quarters"—he paused weightily—"that a baronetcy will be conferred upon me, in that event!"

"Yes?"

The tone betrayed an absolute lack of attention. She had once been used to take a keen interest in his occupations;

to be cast down by his failures and elated by his successes. Had that enthusiasm constituted the greater part of her charm? In its absence Daymond began to find her—must it be confessed?—but indifferent company.

In the embarrassment that momentarily stiffened him, an old habit came to his rescue. Before he knew it, he had taken a cigar from a silver box upon the writing table, and was saying, with the politely apologetic accent of the would-be smoker:

"May I? You used not to mind!"

She made a gesture of assent. As the first rings of bluish vapour mounted into the air, Daymond found her watching him with those intent, expectant eyes.

Feeling himself bound to make some observation, he said: "It is very wonderful to me to see you here! It was very good of you to come!"

She returned: "They had to let me come, I think! I begged so—I prayed so, that at last—" She paused. Daymond was not listening. He was looking at her steadfastly and pondering . . .

It had been his whim, in the first poignancy of bereavement, to destroy all portraits of her, so that with the lapse of years no faulty touch should betray the memory of her vanished beauty. It struck him now for the first time that his brush had played the courtier, and flattered her, for the most part, unblushingly. He found himself criticising unfavourably the turn of her throat and the swell of her bosom, and the dark voluptuous languishment of her look. The faint perfume of heliotrope that was shaken forth now, as of old time, from her hair and her garments no longer intoxicated, but sickened him. This, then, was the woman he had mourned for fifteen years! He began to feel that he had murmured unwisely at the dispensation of Providence. He began to revolt at this recrudescence of an outworn

48

passion—to realise that at twenty-five he had taken a commonplace woman for a divinity—a woman whom, if she had not died when she did, he would have wearied of—ended perhaps in hating. He found himself in danger of hating her now.

"At last they let me come. They said I should repent it—as if I could!" Her eyes rested on him lingeringly; her hand stilled the eager trembling of her lips. "Never! Of course, you seemed a little strange at first. You are not quite—not quite yourself now; it is natural—after fifteen years. And presently, when I tell you—Oh! what will you say when I tell you all?"

She left her chair and came toward him, so swiftly that he had not time to avoid her. She laid her hand on his shoulder and bent her mouth to his ear. One of her peculiarities had been that her lips were always cold, even when her passion burned most fiercely. The nearness of those lips, once so maddeningly desirable and sweet, made Daymond's flesh creep horribly. He breathed with difficulty, and the great drops of agony stood thickly on his forehead—not with weak, superstitious terror of the ghost; with unutterable loathing of the woman.

"Listen!" she said. "They are wise in the place I came from; they know things that are not known here . . . You have heard it said that once in the life of every human being living upon earth comes a time when the utterance of a wish will be followed by its fulfilment. The poor might be made rich, the sick well, the sad merry, the loveless beloved—in one moment—if they could only know when that moment comes! But not once in a million million lifetimes do they hit upon it; and so they live penniless and in pain, and sorrowful and lonely, all their lives. I let my chance go by, like many others, long before I died; but yours is yet to come." Her voice thrilled with a note of wild triumph; the clasp of her arm tightened on his neck. "Oh, love!" she cried; "the wonderful moment is close at hand! It is midnight now"—she pointed to the great north window, through which the frosty silver face of the moon was staring in relief against a framed-in square of velvet blackness, studded with twinkling star-points—"but with the first signs of the dawn that you and I have greeted together, heart of my heart!—how many times in the days that may come again!—with the greying of the East and the paling of the stars comes the Opportunity for you. Now, DO YOU UNDERSTAND?"

He understood and quailed before her. But she was blindly confident in his truth, stupidly reliant on his constancy.

"When it comes, beloved, you shall take me in your arms—breathe your wish upon these lips of mine, in a kiss. Say, while God's ear is open, 'Father, give her back to me, living and loving, as of old!' and I shall be given—I shall be given!"

She threw both arms about him and leaned to him, and sobbed and laughed with the rapture of her revelation and the anticipation of the joy that was to come.

"Remember, you must not hesitate, or the golden chance will pass beyond recall, and I shall go back whence I came, never more to return—never more to clasp you, dearest one, until you die too, and come to me (are you cold, that you shudder so?)—and be with me for always. Listen, listen!"

As she lifted her hand the greatest of all the great clock voices of London spoke out the midnight hour. As other voices answered from far and near Daymond shuddered, and put his dead love from him, and rose up trembling and ghastly pale.

They moved together to the window, and stood looking out. The weather was about to change; the snow was melting, the thaw-drip plashed heavily from roof gutters and balconies, cornices and window ledges. As she laid her hand once more upon his shoulder the stars began to fade out one by one, and in a little while from then the eastward horizon quivered with the first faint throes of dawn.

"Wish!" she cried. "Now! now! before it is too late!" She moved as if to throw herself again upon his breast; but he thrust her from him with resolute hands that trembled no more.

"I wish," he said very distinctly, "to be Sir Robert Daymond, Baronet, and President of the —— before the year is out!"

She fell away from him, and waned, and became unsubstantial and shadowy like the ghost she was, and unlike the thing of flesh and blood she had seemed before. Nothing remained to her of lifelikeness but the scorn and anger, the anguish and reproach of her great eyes.

"Only the dead are faithful to Love—because they are dead," she said. "The living live on—and forget! They may remember sometimes to regret us—beat their breasts and call upon our names—but they shudder if we answer back across the distance; and if we should offer to come back, 'Return!' they say! 'go and lie down in the comfortable graves we have made you; there is no room for you in your old places any more!' They told me I should be sorry for coming; but I would not listen, I had such confidence. I am wiser now! Good-bye!"

A long sigh fluttered by him in the semi-obscurity, like a bird with a broken wing. There was a rattling of curtain rings, the dull sough of falling tapestry, and the opening and closing of a door. She was gone! And Daymond, waking from strangely dreamful slumbers to the cheerlessness of dying embers and burned-out candle, rang the bell for his servant, and ordered lights. A few minutes later saw him, perfectly dressed, stepping into his cab.

"Chesterfield Gardens, Mayfair," he said, giving the direction to his valet for transference to the groom.

"Beg pardon, sir, but Lady Mary Fraber's servant is still waiting!" The man pointed back to the house.

"Ah!" said Daymond, who had had a passing glimpse of alien cord gaiters reposing before his hall-fire. "Tell him I have taken the answer to his mistress myself."

And as he spoke he scattered a handful of torn-up squares of paper—the fragments of a letter—in largesse to the night and the gusty weather.

Lady Clanbevan's Baby

There was a grey, woolly October fog over Hyde Park. The railings wept grimy tears, and the damp yellow leaves dropped soddenly from the soaked trees. Pedestrians looked chilled and sulky; camphor chests and cedar-presses had yielded up their treasures of sables and sealskin, chinchilla and silver fox. A double stream of fashionable traffic rolled west and east, and the rich clarets and vivid crimsons of the automobiles burned through the fog like genial, warming fires.

A Baby-Bunting six horse-power petrol-car, in colour a chrysanthemum yellow, came jiggeting by. The driver stopped. He was a technical chemist and biologist of note and standing, and I had last heard him speak from the platform of the Royal Institution.

"I haven't seen you," said the Professor, "for years."

"That must be because you haven't looked," said I, "for I have both seen and heard you quite recently. Only you were upon the platform and I was on the ground-floor."

"You are too much upon the ground-floor now," said the Professor, with a shudder of a Southern European at the dampness around and under foot, "and I advise you to accept a seat in my car."

And the Baby-Bunting, trembling with excitement at being in the company of so many highly-varnished electric Victorias and forty horse-power auto-cars, joined the steadily-flowing stream going west.

"I wonder that you stoop to petrol, Professor," I said, as the thin, skilful hand in the baggy chamois glove manipulated the driving-wheel, and the little car snaked in and out like a torpedo-boat picking her way between the giant warships of a Channel Squadron.

The Professor's black brows unbent under the cap-peak, and his thin, tightly-gripped lips relaxed into a mirthless smile.

"Ah, yes; you think that I should drive my car by radio-activity, is it not? And so I could—and would, if the pure radium chloride were not three thousand times the price of gold. From eight tons of uranium ore residues about one gramme—that is fifteen grains—can be extracted by fusing the residue with carbonates of soda, dissolving in hydrochloric acid, precipitating the lead and other metals in solution by the aid of hydrogen-sulphide, and separating from the chlorides that remain—polonium, actinium, barium, and so forth—the chloride of radium. With a single pound of this I could not only drive an auto-car, my friend"—his olive cheek warmed, and his melancholy dark eyes grew oddly lustrous—"I could stop the world!"

"And supposing it was necessary to make it go on again?" I suggested.

"When I speak of the world," exclaimed the Professor, "I do not refer to the planet upon which we revolve; I speak of the human race which inhabits it."

"Would the human race be obliged to you, Professor?" I queried.

The Professor turned upon me with so sudden a verbal *riposte* that the Baby-Bunting swerved violently.

"You are not as young as you were when I met you first. To be plain, you are getting middle-aged. Do you like it?"

"I hate it!" I answered, with beautiful sincerity.

"Would you thank the man who should arrest, not the beneficent passage of Time, which means progress, but the wear and tear of nerve and muscle, tissue, and bone, the slow deterioration of the blood by the microbes of old age, for Metchnikoff has shown that there is no difference between the atrophy of senility and the atrophy caused by microbe poison? Would you thank him—the man who should do that for you? Tell me, my friend."

I replied, briefly and succinctly: "Wouldn't I?"

"Ha!" exclaimed the Professor, "I thought so!"

"But I should have liked him to have begun earlier," I said. "Twenty-nine is a nice age, now . . . It is the age we all try to stop at, and can't, however much we try. Look there!"

A Landau limousine, dark blue, beautifully varnished, nickel-plated, and upholstered in cream-white leather, came gliding gracefully through the press of vehicles. From the crest upon the panel to the sober workmanlike livery of the chauffeur, the turn-out was perfection. The pearl it contained was worthy of the setting.

"Look there?" I repeated, as the rose-cheeked, sapphire-eyed, smiling vision passed, wrapped in a voluminous coat of chinchilla and silver fox, with a toque of Parma violets under the shimmer of the silken veil that could only temper the burning glory of her wonderful Renaissance hair.

"There's the exception to the rule . . . There's a woman who doesn't need the aid of Science or of Art to keep her at nine and twenty. There's a woman in whom 'the wear and tear of nerve and muscle, tissue and bone' goes on—if it does go on—imperceptibly. Her blood doesn't seem to be much deteriorated by the microbe of old age, Professor, does it? And she's forty-three! The alchemistical forty-three, that turns the gold of life back into lead! The gold remains gold in her case, for that hair, that complexion, that figure, are," I solemnly declared, "her own."

At that moment Lady Clanbevan gave a smiling gracious nod to the Professor, and he responded with a cold, grave bow. The glow of her gorgeous hair, the liquid sapphire of her eyes, were wasted on this stony man of science. She passed, going home to Stanhope Gate, I suppose, in which neighbourhood she has a house; I had barely a moment to notice the white-bonneted, blue-cloaked nurse on the front of the Landau, holding a bundle of laces and cashmeres, and to reflect that I have never yet seen Lady Clanbevan taking the air out of the society of a baby, when the Professor spoke:

"So Lady Clanbevan is the one woman who has no need of the aid of Art or Science to preserve her beauty and maintain her appearance of youth? Supposing I could prove to you otherwise, my friend, what then?"

"I should say," I returned, "that you had proved what everybody else denies. Even the enemies of that modern Ninon de l'Enclos, who has just passed—"

"With the nurse and the baby?" interpolated the Professor.

"With the nurse and the baby," said I. "Even her enemies—and they are legion—admit the genuineness of the charms they detest. Mentioning the baby, do you know that for twenty years I have never seen Lady Clanbevan out without a baby? She must have quite a regiment of children—children of all ages, sizes, and sexes."

"Upon the contrary," said the Professor, "she has only one!"

"The others have all died young, then?" I asked sympathetically, and was rendered breathless by the rejoinder:

"Lady Clanbevan is a widow."

"One never asks questions about the husband of a professional beauty," I said. "His individuality is merged in hers from the day upon which her latest photograph assumes a marketable value. Are you sure there isn't a Lord Clanbevan alive somewhere?"

"There is a Lord Clanbevan alive," said the Professor coldly. "You have just seen him, in his nurse's arms. He is the only child of his mother, and she has been a widow for nearly twenty years! You do not credit what I assert, my friend?"

"How can I, Professor?" I asked, turning to meet his full face, and noticed that his dark, somewhat opaque brown irises had lights and gleams of carbuncle-crimson in them. "I have had Lady Clanbevan and her progeny under my occasional observation for years. The world grows older, if she doesn't, and she has invariably a baby—*toujours* a new baby—to add to the charming illusion of young motherhood which she sustains so well. And now you tell me that she is a twenty years' widow with one child, who must be nearly of age—or it isn't proper. You puzzle me painfully!"

"Would you care," asked the Professor after a moment's pause, "to drive back to Harley Street with me? I am, as you know, a vegetarian, so I will not tax your politeness by inviting you to lunch. But I have something in my laboratory I should wish to show you."

"Of all things, I should like to come," I said. "How many times haven't I fished fruitlessly for an invitation to visit the famous laboratory where nearly twenty years ago—"

"I traced," said the Professor, "the source of phenomena which heralded the evolution of the Röntgen Ray and the ultimate discovery of the radio-active salt they have christened radium. I called it protium twenty years ago, because of its various and protean qualities. Why did I not push on—perfect the discovery and anticipate Sir

William C— and the X—'s? There was a reason. You will understand it before you leave my laboratory."

The Baby-Bunting stopped at the unfashionable end of Harley Street, in front of the dingy yellow house with the black front door, flanked by dusty boxes of mildewed dwarf evergreens, and the Professor, relieved of his fur-lined coat and cap, led the way upstairs as lightly as a boy. Two garret-rooms had been knocked together for a laboratory. There was a tiled furnace at the darker end of the long skylighted room thus made, and solid wooden tables much stained with spilt chemicals, were covered with scales, glasses, jars, and retorts—all the tools of chemistry. From one of the many shelves running round the walls, the Professor took down a circular glass flask and placed it in my hands. The flask contained a handful of decayed and mouldy-looking wheat, and a number of peculiarly offensive-looking little beetles with tapir-like proboscises.

"The perfectly developed beetle of the *Calandria granaria*," said the Professor, as I cheerfully resigned the flask, "a common British weevil, whose larvae feed upon stored grain. Now look at this." He reached down and handed me a precisely similar flask, containing another handful of grain, cleaner and sounder in appearance, and a number of grubs, sharp-ended chrysalis-like things buried in the grain, inert and inactive.

"The larvae of *Calandria granaria*," said the Professor, in his drawling monotone. "How long does it take to hatch the beetle from the grub you ask? Less than a month. The perfect weevils that I have just shown you I placed in their flask a little more than three weeks back. The grubs you see in the flask you are holding, and which, as you will observe by their anxiety to bury themselves in the grain so as to avoid contact with the light, are still immature, I placed in the glass receptacle twenty years ago. Don't drop the flask—I value it."

"Professor!" I gasped.

"Twenty years ago," repeated the Professor, delicately handling the venerable grubs, "I enclosed these grubs in this flask, with sufficient grain to fully nourish them and bring them to the perfect state. In another flask I placed a similar number of grubs in exactly the same quantity of wheat. Then for twenty-four hours I exposed flask number one to the rays emanating from what is now called radium. And as the electrons discharged from radium are obstructed by collision with air-atoms, I exhausted the air contained in the flask." He paused.

"Then, when the grubs in flask number two hatched out," I anticipated, "and the larvae in flask number one remained stationary, you realised—"

"I realised that the rays from the salt arrested growth, and at the same time prolonged to an almost incalculable extent," said the Professor—"for you will understand that the grubs in flask number one had lived as grubs half a dozen times as long as grubs usually do . . . And I said to myself that the discovery presented an immense, a tremendous field for future development. Suppose a young woman of, say, twenty-nine were enclosed in a glass receptacle of sufficient bulk to contain her, and exposed for a few hours to my protium rays, she would retain for many years to come—until she was a great-grandmother of ninety!—the same charming, youthful appearance—"

"As Lady Clanbevan!" I cried, as the truth rushed upon me and I grasped the meaning this astonishing man had intended to convey.

"As Lady Clanbevan presents to-day," said the Professor, "thanks to the discovery of a—"

"Of a great man," said I, looking admiringly at the lean worn figure in the closely-buttoned black frock-coat.

"I loved her . . . It was a delight to her to drag a disciple of science at her chariot-wheels. People talked of me as a coming man. Perhaps I was . . . But I did not thirst for distinction, honours, fame . . . I thirsted for that woman's love . . . I told her of my discovery—as I told her everything. Bah!" His lean nostrils worked. "You know the game that is played when one is in earnest and the other at play. She promised nothing, she walked delicately among the passions she sowed and fostered in the souls of men, as a beautiful tigress walks among the poison-plants of the jungle. She saw that rightly used, or wrongly used, my great discovery might save her beauty, her angelic, dazzling beauty that had as yet but felt the first touch of Time. She planned the whole thing, and when she said, 'You do not love me if you will not do this', I did it. I was mad when I acceded to her wish, perhaps; but she is a woman to drive men frenzied. You have seen how coldly, how slightingly she looked at me when we encountered her in the Row? I tell you—you have guessed already—I went there to see her. I always go where she is to be encountered, when she is in town. And she bows, always; but her eyes are those of a stranger. Yet I have had her on her knees to me. She cried and begged and kissed my hands."

He knotted his thin hands, their fingers brown-tipped with the stains of acids, and wrung and twisted them ferociously.

"And so I granted what she asked, carried out the experiment, and paid what you English call the piper. The giant glass bulb with the rubber-valve door was blown and finished in France. It involved an expense of three hundred pounds. The salt I used—of protium (christened radium now)—cost me all my savings—over two thousand pounds—for I had been a struggling man—"

"But the experiment?" I broke in. "Good Heavens, Professor! How could a living being remain for any time in an exhausted receiver? Agony unspeakable, convulsions, syncope, death! One knows what the result would be. The merest common sense—"

"The merest common sense is not what one employs to make discoveries or carry out great experiments," said the Professor. "I will not disclose my method; I will only admit to you that the subject—the subjects were insensible; that I induced anaesthesia by the ordinary ether-pump apparatus, and that the strength of the ray obtained was concentrated to such a degree that the exposure was complete in three hours." He looked about him haggardly. "The experiment took place here nineteen years ago—nineteen years ago, and it seems to me as though it were yesterday."

"And it must seem like yesterday to Lady Clanbevan—whenever she looks in the glass," I said. "But you have pricked my curiosity, Professor, by the use of the plural. Who was the other subject?"

"Is it possible you don't guess?" The sad, hollow eyes questioned my face in surprise. Then they turned haggardly away. "My friend, the other subject associated with Lady Clanbevan in my great experiment was—Her Baby!"

I could not speak. The dowdy little grubs in the flask became for me creatures imbued with dreadful potentialities . . . The tragedy and the sublime absurdity of the thing I realised caught at my throat, and my brain grew dizzy with its horror.

"Oh! Professor!" I gurgled, "how—how grimly, awfully, tragically ridiculous! To carry about with one wherever one goes a baby that never grows older—a baby—"

"A baby nearly twenty years old? Yes, it is as you say, ridiculous and horrible," the Professor agreed.

"What could have induced the woman!" burst from me.

The Professor smiled bitterly.

"She is greedy of money. It is the only thing she loves—except her beauty and her power over men; and during the boy's infancy—that word is used in the Will—she has full enjoyment of the estate. After he 'attains to manhood'—I quote the Will again—hers is but a life-interest. Now you understand?"

I did understand, and the daring of the woman dazzled me. She had made the Professor doubly her tool.

"And so," I gurgled between tears and laughter, "Lord Clanbevan, who ought to be leaving Eton this year to commence his first Oxford term, is being carried about in the arms of a nurse, arrayed in the flowing garments of a six-months' baby! What an astonishing conspiracy!"

"His mother," continued the Professor calmly, "allows no one to approach him but the nurse. The family are only too glad to ignore what they consider a deplorable case of atavistic growth-arrest, and the boy himself—" He broke off. "I have detained you," he said, after a pause. "I will not do so longer. Nor will I offer you my hand. I am as conscious as you are—that it has committed a crime." And he bowed me out with his hands sternly held behind him. There were few more words between us, only I remember turning on the threshold of the laboratory, where I left him, to ask whether protium—radium, as it is now christened—checks the growth of every organic substance? The answer I received was curious:

"Certainly, with the exception of the nails and the hair!"

A week later the Professor was found dead in his laboratory . . . There were reports of suicide—hushed up. People said he had been more eccentric than ever of late, and theorised about brain-mischief; only I located the trouble in the heart. A year went by, and I had almost forgotten Lady Clanbevan—for she went abroad after the Professor's death—when at a little watering-place on the Dorset coast, I saw that lovely thing, as lovely as ever—she who was fifty if a day! With her were the blue-cloaked elderly nurse and Lord Clanbevan, borne, as usual, in the arms of his attendant, or wheeled in a luxurious perambulator. Day after day I encountered them—the lovely mother, the middle-aged nurse, and the mysterious child—until the sight began to get on my nerves. Had the Professor selected me as the recipient of a secret unrivalled in the records of biological discovery, or had he been the victim of some maniacal delusion that cold October day when we met in Rotten Row? One peep under the thick white lace veil with which the baby's face was invariably covered would clear everything up! Oh! for a chance to allay the pangs of curiosity!

The chance came. It was a hot, waspy August forenoon. Everybody was indoors with all the doors and windows open, lunching upon the innutritive viands alone procurable at health resorts—everybody but myself, Lord Clanbevan, and his nurse. She had fallen asleep upon a green-painted esplanade seat, gratuitously shielded by a striped awning. Lord Clanbevan's C-springed, white-hooded, cane-built perambulator stood close beside her. He was, as usual, a mass of embroidered cambric and cashmere, and, as always, thickly veiled, his regular breathing heaved his infant breast; the thick white lace drapery attached to his beribboned bonnet obscured the features upon which I so ardently longed to gaze! It was the chance, as I have said; and as the head of the blue-cloaked nurse dropped reassuringly upon her breast, as she emitted the snore that gave assurance of the soundness of her slumbers, I stepped silently on the gravel towards the baby's perambulator. Three seconds, and I stood over its apparently sleeping inmate; another, and I had lifted the veil from the face of the mystery—and dropped it with a stifled cry of horror!

The child had a moustache!

Peter

*An Episode in the Life
of Pierrot and Pierrette*

Pierrot and Pierrette fell in love. That was to be expected, Pierrots and Pierrettes always do. But Pierrette and Pierrot got married, which is rather unusual: and they had a family, which I never before heard of—in the case of a Pierrot and Pierrette.

The family was only one in number, a little boy, who was serious-minded from the very beginning, though you would have thought the baby belonging to such a married pair must necessarily be a kind of joyful imp. Pierre was his Christian name, but he liked Peter best; which shows the sort of child he was.

He was pale and peaky, with large, grave, dark eyes. They were eyes that, from the first, asked questions, reflected thoughts, and criticised. Peter wondered why his parents wore white sugar-loaf hats and neck-frills, and why mother's skirts were so short and the pompons on her shoes so large. His father's long white blouse and baggy trousers, trimmed with pompons like those on Madame Pierrette's shoes, puzzled and worried him. Other little boys' fathers wore coats and trousers, creaky boots, and silk hats or bowlers, gold watches that ticked were in their pockets, and they wore shirts with collars, and neckties with pins. He wished his own father could be like them, with a sensible red or brown face, not one chalked all over white.

Peter wondered why he was not washed and dressed, made to learn, and let play like other people's little Peters. To be carried in the pocket of his father's baggy trousers and pulled out like a kitten or a rabbit in the middle of some stage scene was a great trial to him. He hated being loaded into cannon and fired off, used as the top of a human pyramid, handed and bandied about or tossed like a ball from one person to another. It was neither comfortable nor dignified. Grown-up people sat in the theatre and laughed to see it done, but they would not have done it to their own little boys, nor, though all the little boys screamed with delight and clapped their hands at the sight of Peter's queer usage, would they have liked to be treated in that way.

"They'd cry, and kick and bite—they would!" Peter said to himself, "and why don't I? I wonder?"

He was always wondering, poor little Peter with the serious mind. But, most of all, he wondered why his parents—who had sweet voices and sang duets to the mandoline, *Au Clair de la Lune* and *Minette*, and other things—so that people applauded and asked for more—he wondered why, even at home, they preferred to converse in dumb show?

"Are you hungry, Peter?" Why couldn't father just ask that, instead of opening his mouth as wide as a red letter-box, and pointing down it, rubbing the front of his blouse with the palm of the other hand and chucking Peter under the chin with the toe of his left foot.

"Are you sleepy, Peter?" Why couldn't mother just ask *that*, instead of pretending to go to sleep with the palm of her hand for a pillow and then stroking Peter's face from the forehead down to the chin? It was so unreasonable, and took up so much more time, Peter couldn't help wondering . . .

There was another wonder, too, that gave him much pain. He had learned to read, and, of course, took to the newspapers, which his parents only read when they contained notices of their own performances. When there weren't any notices, they said (in eloquent signs) that there was nothing in the papers; when there were bad notices, Pierrot used to signify that the critics were silly fellows, who did not know their business. When the notices were good, out came the mandolines and the bottle of *vin ordinaire*, and there were smoked sausages and Brie cheese for supper. Peter couldn't bear sausages or cheese, because, with legs of mutton, they were just the things that, on the stage at the theatre, Pierrot stole from various people, while hundreds of others looked on. It made Peter feel sick to read in the newspapers how many people were sent to prison for doing these things, and you may guess that it was not very long before he fell sick in bad earnest. His eyes were very bright and much too big, his feet felt light, and his head hot and large and heavy, and at night, when he laid it on the pillow of his little white bed, so many wheels seemed to be whirring round inside that he was glad to lift it up again. But by and by came a day when he could not lift it up at all! Oh! poor little Peter, who was too young and weak to bear so much wondering! Then Pierrette fell down on both knees at the left side of the pillow, and Pierrot on one knee at the right, and they clutched at their hearts with anxious gestures, and wrung their hands to signify despair. Then Pierrot slapped his forehead, and Pierrette clapped her hands, for she knew her husband had had an idea. When Pierrot had hobbled, leaning on a gold-headed cane, across the room, taken imaginary snuff and felt Peter's pulse, Pierrette knew that the doctor ought to be called in.

So the doctor was sent for, and came. He was quite unlike Pierrot's doctor, a brisk, sturdy, middle-aged gentleman, with kind eyes. He shook his head when he touched the little wasted hand Peter held out to him, and said, "This should have been seen to before. You had better send him to the Children's Hospital." But Pierrette screamed and fainted, and Pierrot slapped his forehead and moaned in agony at the idea, and then upset the salts all over Pierrette, and Pierrette came to and boxed Pierrot's ears, and there was such a to-do that the doctor was glad to get away, saying as he left, "You professional people are all nerves and no brains. If you won't send him, you won't! but he *would* have had a chance if you had! Now . . . but I'll look in again. Get the prescription made up, give the medicine regularly, keep quiet if you can, don't worry him."

With these parting injunctions the doctor was gone. Pierrot emptied his pockets on the little bed, and found he had only eleven pence. Pierrette uttered a cry of agony. Then they fell into each other's arms and wept, and then the clock struck, and they took their bundle and started for the theatre. Peter did not get the medicine but the quiet of the empty room did almost as much good.

He dozed a little. Then—something made him open his eyes. On a chair by the bed, with her face turned towards him, sat a tall, wonderful lady. She wore a gown of neutral brown, made high and simply fitting, but the grand sweep of her shoulders and the splendid pillar of her throat showed the beauty of her form, even to a child's eyes. Her face was full of sunlight and of shadow, and her eyes were grey and tender, and deep as mountain lakes. The sorrow of all the world and all its joy seemed to have rolled over her like waves, and, when she smiled, Peter felt that the sweetness of it was more than he could bear. She stooped over him and took him in her arms and cherished him, and he asked, with her lips upon his eyelids and his head upon her bosom—

"Please, why did you never come before?"

She said, and her voice was like the hush of the wind amongst the pine-tops, and the breaking of waves upon a sunset shore—

"Because you never wanted me so much."

"Please take me back with you!" said Peter.

"Oh! then, I must," she said, "for when a child asks for that it is always granted. But your father and mother, Peter—will they not grieve?"

"Not so much," said old young Peter wisely, "if you will give them something to play with instead of me. A poodle, that can sit up and lie dead."

She laughed very softly and yet clearly, as a thrush laughs, swinging on the topmost bough of a cherry tree in the dawning of a bright June day, and the corners of her eyes crinkled so like the corners of her lips that Peter wanted to kiss them as well.

"They shall have the poodle," she said.

So the lovely, wonderful lady promised that Pierrot and Pierrette should have a clever poodle instead of Peter, and Peter was glad, because he knew now they would not fret long about him. A poodle would suit them so much better than a little boy.

Then the lady gathered Peter in her arms and rose to go, and then her dark dress became white and shiny, and such a radiance streamed from her eyes and shone in her face as she looked at Peter, that he smiled for joy, and said—

"Are you a fairy, please?" For Pierrot had told him about the fairies in the Christmas pantomime.

"I am Death," the lady said, and carried him away to a land more glorious and happy than Peter had ever dreamed of.

❧

When Pierrot and Pierrette came home from the theatre—very late, for they had forgotten Peter and supped with a friend—they found their little boy gone. In his place, sitting upright on the little bed, was a great white poodle. The dog looked knowing, and the moon, that peeped in through the window of the garret where Pierrot and Pierrette lived, looked wise.

"My child, my boy!" cried Pierrette in dumb show; "somebody has stolen him!"

"Let us travel through the wide world until we find him!" gestured Pierrot, throwing on a cloak and taking a walking-stick as he extended the other hand to Pierrette.

The poodle sat up. Pierrot began to laugh.

"That is certainly an intelligent animal," said he.

"Ask it where Peter is?" suggested Pierrette.

Pierrot did, and the beast lay dead. It was clearly no use to seek for Peter.

So Pierrot, Pierrette, and the poodle lived together all their lives. Neither Pierrot nor Pierrette ever knew what had become of Peter, but the poodle was wiser than they.

Clairvoyance

"Let's get through with the correspondence, there's a love!" urged Miss Predicta. "I've six important appointments to read the future between eleven-thirty and lunch, besides the chance callers that may drop in. By the way, what do you think of the new door-plate, 'Predicta' in big black letters, and nothing else?"

"The most strikingest thing in the line I ever see, Jenny dear!" said the typist, clicking back the bar and ringing a little bell, as she slid a sheet of paper into the machine.

" 'Most striking', please; and don't call me Jenny in business hours," said Miss Predicta freezingly. Then she dictated:

BOND STREET.

MADAME,—

We regret to hear that the crystal supplied does not show coming events as clearly as you could wish. We are quite ready on its return, accompanied by your cheque or P.O. for ten shillings extra, to supply the more expensive Himalayan article, as used by the leading Mahatmas.

"Be careful about your spelling, as this is a doctor's wife in a country town. If she was a Duchess it wouldn't matter!" said Miss Predicta.

"That word always bothers me," said the typist, stopping to use the India-rubber. "Six different ways I've spelt Mahatma—in one letter alone—and not one of 'em turned out right. But you always was the clever one of us two, in spelling and everything else. There's the client's bell, Jenny dear!"

"Jenny dear" jumped up as a telephone-bell whirred, and, unhooking the receiver, listened to the wiry voice that came from the ground-floor.

"C.C.S.A.T.L.L.C.," ticked the telephone in Miss Predicta's private alphabetical cypher-code.

"Casual Caller, Swell About Town, Looks Like Cash," translated Miss Predicta mentally. She glided between the plush curtains into the bower of mystery, and had barely time to fall upon a chair painted with cabalistic characters and plunge into a profound reverie before the Casual Caller appeared. He was tall, tawny, square-shouldered, attired in accurately cut morning tweeds, and brought with him the last whiff of the Havana thrown away upon Miss Predicta's threshold.

"Haw!" said he, with an air of polite embarrassment. "I was told—that is—"

His eye took in an interior chastely draped and decorated in red, carefully screened from the light of day, and illuminated by an electric star in the ceiling.

"Haw!" he said again.

Miss Predicta opened her eyes, two deep blue wells of mystery, and pushed a chestnut-tinted mass of carefully disarranged hair from her brow. Robed in a black velvet tea-gown trimmed with cheap imitation point, she certainly looked spiritual, if not mystical.

"You wished to know something of what the Future holds in store for you, sir?"

" 'Pon my word!" said the Casual Caller, putting a well-groomed hard felt hat on the little centre table covered with a cabalistic cloth, "I can't quite say. Your door-plate caught my eye in passing. A young man—pimply boy rather—asked me to walk in, and then said the charge was half-a-crown to see the clairvoyante."

"To see the clairvoyante. But our fee for reading the Future is half-a-guinea," said Miss Predicta.

"The matter with my future is—it's painfully clear," said the Casual Caller, thoughtfully.

"Army," ticked off Miss Predicta, mentally noting the regimental colours of his tie, the tanned muscular hands, and the white strip of forehead above the healthy sunburn of his pleasant countenance.

"Originally *magasin*," silently observed the Casual Caller. "Millinery or Mantles. Had ambitions . . . Wonder who helped her to this start?"

"If you were about to engage in any enterprise, the clairvoyante might advise," said Miss Predicta.

"Mine is not," said the Casual Caller gravely, "an enterprising disposition."

"Or if you wanted to invest money! . . . Bet on a race, for instance," Miss Predicta hazarded.

"Do you foretell winners?" the Casual Caller asked with interest.

"Occasionally," said Miss Predicta, guardedly.

"It must spoil a man's fun to know beforehand that his beast is going to tootle in Number One," said the Casual Caller. "No; I don't think I'll invest to-day."

"We supply horoscopes, character and marriage charts," said Miss Predicta, alluringly, "at reasonable prices."

"Suppose a husband steers by one of your marriage charts, and strikes reef in a spot where none is marked," the Casual Caller queried, "does he sue you for damages, or do you shirk responsibility?"

"We instruct in the science of Hypnotism," said Miss Predicta. "Perhaps you might care to take a course of lessons? Or, if you have lost a relative or dear friend, whom you cannot trace, the clairvoyante might possibly put you on the track."

"By Jove! Now you remind me," said the Casual Caller, "I *have* lost a friend. Quite lately too."

"Then," suggested Miss Predicta, pushing a *papier mâché* skull money-box across the little table, "if you wish to consult the clairvoyante, our charge is ten-and-six." From force of habit she nearly added "three farthings".

"Pretty idea that!" said the Casual Caller, as he extracted half a sovereign and sixpence from his waistcoat pocket and dropped them into the skull. "So cheery!"

He added: "I may presume, then, that I have the pleasure of addressing you as a clairvoyante?"

"Would you kindly remove your hat?" said Miss Predicta, preparing to dive into the future.

"Certainly. I beg your pardon." The Casual Caller transferred his hat to a chair. "You ladies are running us close," he observed. "Nothing for the men to do soon, positively. My sister patronises a lady-chemist; most of the business men I know employ lady secretaries. I sent off a wireless message just now; the operator was a young lady— handed me change for a fiver, two shillings short—with a perfectly charmin' smile. Dropped in at my gunmaker's to be fitted for a new gun, and was measured for a sporting double self-ejectin' breech-loader by a young woman who knocked the clay birds over right and left, quite like a professional shootist. Haw!"

Miss Predicta drew a little wand of black wood with an open hand at the end of it from behind the cushion of her chair. She pointed this at the electric ceiling-star, and with the assistance of a switch under the table the lights became a cheerless blue.

"I say—what!" exclaimed the Casual Caller.

"I must ask you not to talk," said Miss Predicta, severely. "The spirits object to idle conversation," she added.

"In business hours—quite correct!" nodded the Casual Caller.

Miss Predicta, hoping to induce awe, pedalled the foot switch, and the lights went green.

"Do the spirits do that?" inquired the Casual Caller. "Because," he added, as Miss Predicta bowed her head in assent, "I wish you would kindly ask 'em to select a more becoming colour." As the light revolved to rose, he added, "That's awfully nice; thanks such a lot!" and Miss Predicta felt herself blush slightly under the appreciative directness of his gaze. Her hand shook a little as she lighted a pastille in an imitation Satsuma incense-burner.

"Phew! I say, do the spirits really want a smell of that kind?" objected the Casual Caller. "Because, if not—"

Miss Predicta, whose gaze was professionally fixed, made no reply. The pastille sent up a nasty little fume; the roar of Bond Street came through the red curtains . . . Suddenly the Casual Caller sneezed.

"Couldn't help it, upon my word," said he, in muffled tones filtered through a silk handkerchief of the newest shade. "Wonder the spirits stand it, by Jove I do!"

"I must really ask you not to talk!" said Miss Predicta. She placed a crystal ball on an ebony stand upon the table, and snapped the lights out. The crystal shone moonily in the obscurity. "Now think of your lost friend," ordered Miss Predicta in a voice effectively hollow. "Think—and I will gaze in the magic ball and tell you what I see."

The Casual Caller bent over the table. The faces of the inquirer and of the seeress were conjecturally six inches apart. The perfume of excellent cigars, mingled with the blameless odour of clean linen and a twang of Russia leather saluted Miss Predicta's nostrils in agreeable whiffs. The Casual Caller on his part was aware of violet soap, pearl powder, singed hair—Miss Predicta had used the undulators too hot that morning—and the searching fragrance of a sweetmeat dear to him in youth.

"Now tell me your thoughts," said Miss Predicta.

"Do all prophetesses eat peppermints?" asked the Casual Caller.

"You are rude, I must say!" said Miss Predicta huffily.

"You wanted to know what I was thinking," said the Casual Caller apologetically. "And that was what I thought."

"Oh! but you mustn't think about me," said Miss Predicta with some coquetry. "Think about the friend you have lost. Keep on thinking quite hard!"

"I do . . . I am!" said the Casual Caller.

"Man?" queried Miss Predicta, "or woman?"

"She was a dear little thing!" said the Casual Caller. His voice shook.

"Woman!" said Miss Predicta lucidly. "Of what complexion," she added—"blonde or brunette?"

For a moment the Casual Caller did not appear able to reply. The little table shook and the crystal quivered.

"He loves her still," thought Miss Predicta, "no matter how she's treated him. Some people do have luck!" She repeated her interrogation. "Was she dark or fair, or neither the one nor the other—like me?"

The table shook again slightly. Then—"She had brown eyes," said the Casual Caller chokily.

"Did you consider she was very attached?" queried Miss Predicta. "It looks, in the crystal," she added, "as if the love was more on one side than the other. Was she fond of you?"

The Casual Caller replied in muffled tones: "Awfully. Used to go with me everywhere, and, if I happened to go out without her, sit watching for hours for me to come back."

"And did her love die out suddenly?" asked Miss Predicta, peering into the crystal. "There's a blur here that seems like a change. And brown-eyed women are very deceitful."

"I came home one day—" The Casual Caller faltered.

"And found her out?" interrogated Miss Predicta.

"Found her gone," gasped the Casual Caller. The table not only shook, but creaked, and Miss Predicta, who had read in novels of the agony of a strong man in sorrow, swallowed a sigh.

"She had deserted you?" she hinted. "It looks like it—in the crystal!"

"She had broken her chain," said the Casual Caller gloomily, "and bolted out of the house."

"There *was* a chain, then?" the seeress hinted.

"I beg your pardon," said the Casual Caller.

"How long had you been married?" asked Miss Predicta boldly.

"Not long," said the Casual Caller.

"Quite recently?" asked Miss Predicta.

"So recently," said the Casual Caller, "that the affair hasn't come off yet. I happen to be a bachelor. Haw!"

"Oh, I never! . . . You really—" Miss Predicta tingled to her finger-tips with indignation at this shameless effrontery. "So good-looking," she thought, "to be such a wretch!" "But there's a wedding in the crystal," she resumed. "I can see a Bishop's sleeves and a lot of white flowers, and—certainly there's a cake. Yes, without doubt, a cake!"

"Perhaps it's your wedding," said the Casual Caller, "and your cake?"

"It's your future," said Miss Predicta, freezingly. "Did you endeavour to trace her?" she continued, "the poor unhappy creature with the brown eyes who fled from the shelter of your roof when she broke the chain that—you know! Of course, you've tried to trace her?"

"Hunted everywhere," said the Casual Caller. "Advertised. Went round to all my friends' rooms on the chance of tumbling over her."

"Oh!" gasped Miss Predicta. "The idea!"

"That was one of her chief faults. Would go to people's houses she'd taken a fancy to," said the Casual Caller. "Nothing could break her of it!"

Miss Predicta's eyebrows went up under cover of the darkness.

"But when she never turned up I had to come to the conclusion she'd been kidnapped," continued the Casual Caller. "Mothers are hardly likely to run away, you know, when there are two podgy, round-bodied little beggars rolling on the hearthrug and whimpering for her to come back."

"*A* mother," observed Miss Predicta sarcastically, "but some women have no natural feeling. Two innocent babies abandoned! When she might have put 'em into their perambulator, and taken them too! I say it's a shame!"

The table quivered convulsively. In the obscurity Miss Predicta became aware that the Casual Caller had pulled out his handkerchief and was mopping his eyes.

"Th-thank you!" he gasped. "It does seem unnatural, doesn't it? Perhaps you would kindly look into the crystal and try whether you can get a glimpse of her?"

"What was her Christian name?" demanded Miss Predicta, relieved to find that the profligate's better nature was asserting itself at last.

"I called her 'Floss'," gurgled the Casual Caller.

"There was no quarrel previous to her disappearance?" hinted Miss Predicta.

"No. N-no," hesitated the Casual Caller. "Except—but you couldn't call that a quarrel!"

"Couldn't call what?"

"What took place," said the Casual Caller. "I'd told the little beast to fetch my gloves—a thing she'd done thousands of times. She disobeyed me, and I gave her a cut with a riding-cane. That's all!"

"You brute!" rose to Miss Predicta's lips, but she kept the words back with an effort. All her sympathies went out to the woman—the mother, who had suffered outrage at this aristocrat's ruthless hands. She bent over the crystal, resolved to awaken his dormant conscience at the expense of veracity. "Silence, please!" she said. "The shadows begin to clear. Now they move aside. What is this?" At the cue, started by the typist in the next room, a musical box began to discourse the "Shadow Dance" from *Dinorah*.

"I see," continued Miss Predicta, "a lonely road. The figure of a woman, distraught and terror-stricken, recedes into the distance. Her face is turned from me. Now she looks back. She has brown eyes. Was she wearing a sable fur when she disappeared?"

The table rocked violently. After an interval of struggle the Casual Caller managed to say: "No, dog-skin—with a head and one tail."

"They call it European fox," said Miss Predicta severely. She thought he might have bought something better than that for the helpless creature who had sacrificed all for him. Now she lifted her head dramatically as she cried: "The scene changes! I see a garret room with a bed. The same woman lies upon it. A doctor bends over her. A reverend-looking gentleman with white hair enters. Listen—she speaks! '*Tell him that I forgive him,*' she falters—'*him, the author of my misery and ruin!*' " The musical box broke off the "Shadow Dance" and clicked into "Abide with me". " '*Entreat him to take care of my poor, deserted, nameless children!—to marry a better woman!—to see that my grave is kept green, and for the future lead a blameless life!* She sinks back. I hear the death-rattle. All is over! Unhappy Floss is no more!"

Miss Predicta switched up the lights and confronted the crimson face and tear-distilling eyes of the Casual Caller.

"Th-thank you so awf-awfully!" he stammered; "but you've made one mistake. The—the children aren't nameless. One is called 'Waggle' and the other 'Dash'. And Floss happens to be a liver-and-white Clumber spaniel—a Palace Cup winner—I value very much. But I'm uncommonly obliged, all the same. Most interesting *séance!*"

Miss Predicta faced him, with poppy-red cheeks and blazing eyes. The musical box left off before "Amen". "Do you want your money back?" she demanded. "Do you mean to spread about how you came in and guyed—and made a fool of me when I thought—"

"When you thought you were making a fool of me? My dear young lady, don't be alarmed!" said the Casual Caller. "As to injuring you in the clairvoyante business, I shall make a point of sendin' in my friends. If they enjoy themselves as much as I have done—" His shoulders shook again. "But you make one mistake. Shouldn't take it for granted that every man who wears a decent coat and—and necktie is a blackguard. No, by Jove!" He shook his head and put his hat upon it. "Good-morning, Miss—ahem!— Miss Clairvoyante."

Miss Predicta, with tear-blurred vision, saw the Casual Caller on the steps of departure. "Good-morning. And I truly beg your pardon. But whether you forgive me or not," she sighed, "I shall never see you again!"

"Would you care to?" The Causal Caller wheeled upon the threshold of the crimson temple, and as he smiled it seemed to Miss Predicta that the electric light had snapped back to rose. "Would you really? Haw! Because, if so—if you'd really—care to—see me again—you'd better—"

"Better?" gasped Miss Predicta, with a thumping heart.

"Better look into the Magic Crystal!" said the Casual Caller. "Good-day!"

The Compleat Housewife

The Story of a Battaglio Pie

So many male members of the British aristocracy find their feminine complements in American social circles, that I guess I won't astonish any one that reads this when I announce myself, *née* Lydia Randolph, of Savannah—described in Glatt's *Guide to the United States* as "the chief city and commercial metropolis of Georgia"— as a slip of Southern wild orange grafted by marriage upon one of the three-hundred-year-old citron trees that are the pride of the greenhouses at Hindsway Abbey, Deershire.

Bryan—my husband is Sir Bryan Corbryan, sixteenth baronet of that name—was travelling in the Southern States when we met at the Jasper House at Thunderbolt, a fashionable early summer resort on the Warsaw River. I had seen clean-made, springy, red-and-white, handsome Englishmen before, but there was something particularly distinguished about this one, or it seemed so. We were neighbours at the *table d'hôte*, and Sir Bryan had no idea how to eat green corn until I gave him an object lesson, and was wonderfully ignorant about simple things like fried egg-plant. Chicken gumbo reminded him of Indian curries, and he thought our green oysters as good as those of Ostend, but he drew the line at raw canvas-back and roast ices. We became so friendly over the *carte du jour* that Mamie—my second sister—parodied the old rhyme about love—

"Oh, 'tis food, 'tis food, 'tis food
That makes the world go round!"

she sang, as we moved towards the ladies' drawing-room.

"*Grow* round, you mean," said I scornfully, as the elevator carried us upwards, and the coloured boy grinned.

"After all," said Mamie thoughtfully—she is considered a very brainy girl by her school professors—"without food there would be no love. People would just pine and dwindle and die. Wouldn't they, Belvidere?"

"Iss, missus," said the lift-boy, catching and biting the quarter Mamie tossed him.

Well, next day we met Sir Bryan again. After that it was usually me. We all greatly enjoyed that June holiday in our differing ways. Marma simply drank in the restfulness of a hotel with three or four hundred guests in it, after the harassing worries of a household consisting of a husband, three daughters, and seven servants, and rocked and fanned from morning until night. For us young folks there were drives, fishing parties, walking excursions, and bathing sociables. My! the time flew, but the world stood still quite suddenly, or seemed to, when Sir Bryan asked me to be his wife. He said I was the loveliest girl on the Salts or the face of Creation, and he just burned with longing to carry me home as his bride to Deershire, and walk with me under the Tudor oaks he had told me about. Tudor oaks! And a girl whose father was making a corner in cotton on Bay Street at that very moment! But Sir Bryan appeared to see no discrepancy, and that corner in cotton made me quite an heiress, as it afterwards turned out.

Well, our wedding—Bryan's and mine—was solemnised at the Savannah Episcopal Church, fronting Madison Square. It was a jessamine and tuberose wedding, cartloads of those blooms being employed. I had privately begged

Bryan to send home for the first baronet's gold inlaid suit of tilting armour to be married in; but he begged to be excused, as wrought steel is such heavy summer-wear. Otherwise, he thought, considering the almost Presidential amount of handshaking a bridegroom usually has to go through, gauntlets would be rather an advantage than otherwise.

We spent a week of our honeymoon trip at Newport and one on the ocean, and two in that Eden of the modern Adam and Eve, Paris, and then we went home to Deershire and Hindway Abbey, driving the whole way from the station under festoons of parti-coloured flags, while the bells rang peals of welcome, and school children and tenants cheered, and the guard of honour supplied by the Deershire Mounted Volunteers kept up a deafening clatter behind that made the spirited horses more spirited still: and then we turned in between old stone entrance gate-pillars crested with heraldic monsters like those on Bryan's coat-of-arms, and drove along the wide avenue under those Tudor oaks Bryan had talked about, and the Abbey, a glorious old building of ancient red brick faced with white stone, rose up before us, girt with its ancient terraced walks and clipped hedges of yew and holly, and smothered in roses and wisteria to its mossy tiled roofs and the very tips of its twisted chimneys.

"Oh," I cried to Bryan, "never tell me that gentlemen in trunks and ladies in farthingales, or *beaux* in powdered periwigs and laced brocade coats, and belles in hoops and furbelows don't promenade here in the witching hours of night under the glimpses of the waning moon, because I simply shan't believe you!"

"So you like it?" said my husband, looking pleased and proud.

"Like it!" was all I could say; but it seemed enough for Bryan. He took my hand and led me into our home, and the red light of the great wood fire upon the gleaming hearth-dogs of the old wainscoted hall shone upon two very happy people.

Then—I just hate to think of it!—hard upon all the cheering and curtseying welcome came the blue-enveloped cablegram from Marma, with its brief, sharp, clearly worded message of misfortune. Parpa had had a spell of hemiplegia in consequence of a slump in lumber, which he had tided through, poor dear, at the expense of his health. I cried and begged to go back to the States at any risk, but Bryan was firm. I could see that if I had owned three fathers, all lying in imminent peril, it would have been just the same. He would go, he declared, in my place. Parpa had two daughters on the spot, and a son ought to be an appreciated change.

I loathed to let him go, but I loved him for wanting to. I put my head right down on his dear tweed shoulder and told him so. He lifted up my face and kissed it.

"You'll be brave, little woman"—I am five feet eight—"and, Phee, I know you will take care of your mistress?" he said, looking hard at my coloured maid.

"Bless Grashus, Marsa, co'se I will!" said Phee, with a wide, brilliant smile.

And within two hours my husband had driven from the door of his ancestral dwelling, and I was a grass widow. I made this observation to Phee.

"Lor', honey," said she, "ain' dat heaps better dan bein' de real kin'?"

I had not regarded the situation previously from this point of view, and I could not deny that Phee was in the right. But I cried myself to sleep all the same, and woke feeling pretty cheerful, and when I had bathed and dressed, and breakfasted in the morning-room that looked upon the quaintest of old-world gardens bounded with rose-hedges and centred with a splendid four-faced dial, lifted aloft upon a twisted and carven pillar, adorned with the motto, *Nunc sol nunc umbra*, I received a respectful message from Mrs. Pounds, the housekeeper, asking for an audience.

She was a handsome old lady in a lace cap and rustling black silk gown, and when she had handed me a bunch of keys similar to the bunch that dangled at her waist, she launched into many revelations concerning household affairs, to which I fear I listened absently, being mentally absorbed upon the question of the arrival or non-arrival of Bryan's letter. Joy! a guardedly expressed but distinctly affectionate telegram was handed to me before Mrs. Pounds had got through. Bryan had engaged a deck cabin on the biggest of the Atlantic ferries, and would steam out of Southampton Docks precisely at two PM. A letter was following. Dear telegram! Dear letter! Dearest Bryan! My eyes swam with tears. Oh, how I meant to try to be an ideal wife! How I—

"It being a rainy morning, and unpleasant for walking or driving," I heard Mrs. Pounds say, "and the Abbey being one of the most interesting Tudor residences in the county, perhaps her ladyship would wish to go over the house."

The notion was invigorating.

"Why, certainly!" I exclaimed. "I should just adore to!"

"If her ladyship permits," said Mrs. Pounds, with refrigerating stateliness, "I will act as her ladyship's guide!"

I thanked her and rang for Phee.

"Did her ladyship wish the young black person to attend her?" Mrs. Pounds inquired, with a perfectly glacial stiffness.

"I guess so," I said; "since she is to live in this house, she may as well learn her way about it—the sooner, the better."

"As her ladyship pleases," said Mrs. Pounds, and unhooked her bunch of keys with a shiver of virtuous resignation. Then she said that if her ladyship permitted, she would lead the way, and glided out of the morning-room.

What a refined and subtle pleasure there lies in going over every nook and corner of a noble, ancient house, in traversing the echoing galleries, looking from the mullioned windows upon garden, terrace, alley, pleasaunce, and park, in gazing at ancient pictures painted by inspired hands long since dust, in fingering antique china and glorious old tapestries, tapping ringing corselets and engraven helms, touching gleaming or rusty weapons, looking respectfully on chairs that have upheld historical personages, and carven, canopied beds in which they have slept! That pleasure was to me intensified a thousandfold because the house was Bryan's and mine.

Phee was as enthusiastic in her way as I was, though my way was less ebullient. Her vociferations of "Lordy! Lawd sakes! Bless Grashus!" with other kindred ejaculations, seemed to pain Mrs. Pounds a good deal. But presently that rustling embodiment of respectability threw open a door on the first floor landing of what she termed the west wing, saying—

"This is called Lady Deborah's room, which, although carefully kept free from dust, as her ladyship sees, has never been occupied since the death of Lady Deborah, which occurred of quinsy in the reign of King George the Second, and the lifetime of the tenth baronet, her son. The portrait in oils by Jongmans, set in panel over the chimney-piece, is considered to be a speaking likeness. Her ladyship is wearing the very cap and gown in which she is said to haunt this house, and that book that lies upon the *escritoire* in the window is the identical volume she is said to carry in her hand."

"Fo' de Lawd!" I heard Phee say gutturally behind me.

As for myself, I felt no chill of awe. The triumph of being the mistress of an undeniably ancient, undoubtedly ghost-haunted abbey fired my blood and thrilled my whole being. I advanced to the *escritoire*, an ancient, brass-handled piece of furniture with flowers in Dutch marquetry, and opened the book—a dilapidated volume in brown leather binding—at the title-page. "*The Compleat Housewife*," I read, "*or Accomplished Gentlewoman's Companion. A Collection of Prov'd Recipys in Cookery and Confectionary, With Instructions for the Making of Wines and Cordyals, Also Above 200 Family Specificks, viz. Drinks, Syrups, Salves, Oyntments and Cures for Varyous Distempers. By Eliz. Smith; The Second Edycion. London; Printed for J. Pynkerton agaynst S' Dunstan's Church in Fleet-street in the Reign of His Ma'sty King George II.*"

Phee had backed nervously into the corridor. With the book in my hand, I glanced a friendly *adieu* towards the portrait of Lady Deborah, whose mob-cap and black silk calash encircled a wrinkled yet pleasant and placid countenance, embellished with the fine streakings of rosy red one sees on a good eating apple, and ornamented by huge round spectacles rimmed with silver.

"Thank you," I said to the housekeeper, "but I think I have seen enough for one while. So many stairs are fatiguing to a person accustomed to elevators."

"Her ladyship means lifts?" said Mrs. Pounds, making allowances for the foreigner.

"Not at all," I said. "But I guess you mean elevators." The stout brown leather volume under my arm inspired me to ask a question: "With regard to Lady Deborah, Mrs. Pounds, you will not think it a very odd question if I ask you, have you ever seen her?"

"I will not deceive her ladyship," said the housekeeper. "There have been alarms among the maids and reports circulated by guests long, long before my time, and in my time, but never having viewed the apparition myself, I never gave such credit for an instant. Ghostly hauntings argue unquiet consciences, I have always understood; and what should a virtuous, housekeeping lady, such as Lady Deborah was, by all accounts—and the almshouses she built and endowed are the pride of the village to this day!— have upon her conscience? Her still-room is in the wing, though now turned into a store-room; and my jams, not to say jellies, are made after recipes in ancient writing which I believe to have been hers."

"And this must have been the cookery-book out of which she copied them," said I, glancing into the well-thumbed volume, "which I am going to carry away and look over."

"Oh, my—my lady!" exclaimed Mrs. Pounds, paling slightly and forgetting the third person in her perturbation. "I beg your ladyship's pardon, but your ladyship had best not. They do say—"

"Ah! what do they say?" I asked.

"They say," said Mrs. Pounds, nervously smoothing her muslin apron, "that whenever or however that book is removed from this room, it is always found in its place upon Lady Deborah's *escritoire* next morning. Which would argue, my lady, that she fetches it back herself!"

My Southern blood ran less warmly through my veins, but I held my head up bravely.

"Has any one put that tradition to the test, to your knowledge?" I asked.

Mrs. Pounds pursed her lips and shook her head.

"Very well!" I said in my stateliest manner, and I swept down the corridor, whose ancient oaken planking creaked under my high-heeled French shoes.

It still rained. Two huge fires of apple-wood burned in my great panelled drawing-room, where tall, carved cabinets of Indian ebony, Dutch marquetry, and Chinese lacquer, crowned with lovely vases and bowls of Oriental pottery, stood sentinel on the edges of the worn but beautiful Turkey carpet. I sank into a low, deep chair near the lower hearth-place and stared up at the carvings over the bossed mantelshelf, representing Dante and Beatrice, and other personages from the *Divina Commedia*, all wearing Elizabethan ruffs, trunk hose and farthingales. The rain splashed from the leaden mouths of the lion-headed waterpipes upon the flags of the terrace. It sounded like the tap-tapping of high-heeled brodequins. There was a high-backed, narrow, black oak chair on the opposite edge of the rug, an armless, stiff, uncomfortable chair, and upholstered in gilded leather—or leather that had once been gilded, fastened on with gilt nails, or nails that were once gilt, driven through little round pieces of faded green and red felt. There are articles of furniture that irresistibly evoke in the mind fancy portraits of the people who must have owned them. As I looked at that chair, its outlines became obscure . . . Gradually enormously hooped petticoats of strong, flowered brocade, green with a shrimp-pink pattern of roses, came into view, from the border of which peeped the ends of narrow, square-toed shoes adorned with silver buckles. Languidly and without surprise my eyes travelled from these upwards to the cobweb-lace border of a very fine Swiss—I should say muslin—apron. In the centre of the apron were a pair of withered hands adorned with antique jewelled rings, and covered to the bony knuckles with black silk mittens. I followed the mittens to the lace ruffles of the sleeves, which matched the cinnamon satin peaked bodice—so tightly laced that one could hardly credit a human body being inside—trimmed with heavy silver lace and having puffed paniers on either side. The neck of the bodice was cut square and filled in with soft folds of muslin, and about a withered throat I caught the gleam of a gold and amber necklace. The body I have described ended in the face I had expected. The peaked chin, the pursed-up lips, the withered rose-apple cheeks, slightly pinched nose, and huge silver-rimmed spectacles—all belonged to Lady Deborah's portrait. Almost with gladness I recognised the rolled-up, powdered hair, crowned with the enormous, lappeted mob-cap. It affected me strangely that the old lady did not wear the black silk calash or bonnet, but carried it slung over her thin arm by its wide strings, and that a tortoiseshell-headed cane not represented upon the canvas—a kit-kat—leaned against a little Indian cabinet of striped calamander wood which stood near.

Bryan's family ghost—mine, by virtue of my rights as Bryan's wife! The cold chills and crisping sensations of fear were banished by the pleasant glow of pride which stole over my being as I gazed upon the dear old lady. I had so much regretted Bryan's not having any mother or pleasant elderly women relatives living for me to be cosy and confidential with—and here was one! Not living, but still visible; not to be felt, perhaps, but possibly to be heard. All this while Lady Deborah stared piercingly in my direction. She was not looking at me, but at the open book upon my knee, which had nearly slipped off it, and just as I had made up my mind to venture on a very delicate cough, she spoke, in a dry, rasping old voice—

"Child, if you thought to persuade me you was asleep, you may spare yourself the trouble, for I have seen your eyelids blink these dozen times."

"Oh, Lady Deborah——" I began, but the old lady caught up her cane and rapped me over the knuckles—hard, with the end of it!

"Is that the way you give greeting to your elders, Mistress Impertinence?" she cried shrilly. "Truly, I don't know where the young women are coming to! Dry your eyes, chit!"—they were watering from the smart of my rapped knuckles—"and let me see you make a proper reverence!"

Her cane was hovering. I hastily got out of my chair and made the lowest cotillon-curtsey I had ever achieved.

"Pish!" ejaculated the Lady Deborah Corbryan, with perfectly withering contempt. She waved me aside and rose to her feet. "Fold the arms, thus, cross the legs at the knees, bend them outwards, sink—and recover." She sank as though the floor had opened under her, she recovered—apparently upon the point of vanishing. "Madam," she said, with an agreeable smile which revealed a set of boxwood teeth strung on gold wire, "I vow I am vastly happy to see your ladyship, and venture to hope that your ladyship enjoys good health?"

"Perfectly, thank you. And—dear Lady Deborah—you can't begin to know how real glad I am to see you. I was just expiring to have you drop in!" I stopped, for the old lady's eyes were beginning to snap behind her spectacles.

"Drop in," she said severely, "is not a seemly expression for a young woman. But be seated, child, and tell me your name . . . Lydia Randolph, of Georgia, d'ye say? My young descendant was travelling in the East, I presume, when he encountered you? I hoped, for the honour of the Corbryans, you was a relative of the Grand Turk, or of the Sophy, at least, for our family is very ancient and honourable, let me tell you!"

After an effort or two I gave up the task of trying to persuade Lady Deborah that the State of Georgia was located in America, which she persisted in calling "the Virginias". She was aware that a person named Smith had devoted his life to the exploration and colonisation of New England, and that the English, in 1664, had held possession of New York. She approved of those commodities which came from my country—American rum, cane sugar, coffee, and tobacco—and helped herself to snuff from an amethyst-topped box as she approved.

"My young descendant will take you up to London in the family coach when he returns (I had explained why I figured as a lonely bride) and initiate you into the pleasures of the gay world of fashion," she said. "You must see Mr. Garrick in *Hamlet*, the dear, ingenious man! and Mrs. Siddons as Belvidera—Lud! how she frightened me in her frenzy. And Mr. Johnson—you must see that great, if uncouth, personage—and Mr. Reynolds, the painter—he must be prevailed upon to paint you, for you are not ill-looking, chit, and would be positively handsome was you dressed. Dear me, what junketings I had in my time! . . . Ranelagh, Hampstead, Vauxhall, Marybone Gardens, and Totnam Farm . . . where we went for syllabubs new from the cow—and the *beaux* quarrelled among them which should have the glass I had drank out of. For I was a toast and a beauty, and a sad coquette, too, my dear!" said the old lady, complacently nodding her great cap. "Sir George Cockerell, of Bangwood—a mon'sous rake—tried to carry me off from Bath Wells in a coach with four, in broad day, for which Sir Bryan ran him through, my dear, under the second rib on the left side—and—'You've nicked it, Corbryan,' says Sir George, 'and—and I lose!—but I don't apologise,' and swooned away. And D'Arcy D'Urfée writ a poem upon a pair of fringed gloves I wore at an assembly, and my Lord Chesterfield himself hath paid me compliments. But beauty is a passing flower, child, and so I found it when I took the smallpox and rose from my bed—hung with scarlet cloth, by orders of His Majesty's own physician—to find my face all pitted and my beautiful eyebrows and lashes gone—to a hair!"

"Oh, how dreadful!" I cried. "And—and Sir Bryan?"

"Sir Bryan took to the claret bottle in his sorrow, and to the punch-bowl," said Lady Deborah.

"Drank!" I cried. "Oh, how dreadful!"

"Tush, child!" snapped the old lady. "Don't all our men drink? And our women, too, for that matter! Liquor was made for man, we have the authority of the Ancients upon it! But Sir Bryan took to other things as well—gaming at the Grecian and White's, and other follies—and I was a very unhappy woman for a time. Then I found comfort, chit—in a book with which you are acquainted!"

"The Scriptures, madam?" I said, my lips trembling with sympathy and admiration of the simple piety of the poor, deserted wife.

"My dear mother's Cookery Book. You have it in your lap, child, and by constant study of it I became the most notable housewife in my county . . . Let me trust you have read and pondered its pages," said Lady Deborah, nodding solemnly. " 'Tis as unseemly for a young lady to enter the world without a knowledge of the art of carving, for instance, as to appear at a ball without her sacque and paniers and hooped petticoat. Thou canst unjoint a bittern, I trust? souse a capon, unlace a crane, dismember a heron, lift a swan, and rear a bustard with elegance and discretion?"

"I—I am afraid not," I stammered, keeping the tears back with difficulty as I realised my ignorance of English social customs. "You see, Parpa wished me to be educated in the State where I was raised, and this is my first visit to England. Possibly I could souse a capon, but swans are such vicious things, I should never dare to lift one. And as to rearing a bustard, I've never seen one yet."

"Lydia, I vow you horrify me! No more, child, or I shall have a fit of the spleen!" Lady Deborah fanned herself with the cunningest tortoiseshell fan, and sniffed at a silver apple pricked full of holes that hung from her *châtelaine*. "I shall have to take a dram of gentian wine or carduus-seed bruised in old sack," she added. "Either is sovereign, both for spleen and the vapours. Remember that, should you happen to be attacked by these distempers."

"I'm sure I hope I shan't be!" said I fervently.

"Rue-water is also excellent in fits," said the old lady loftily. "My rue-water was justly celebrated. I distributed it on Thursdays to all the poor who chose to bring bottles to contain it. The juice of the plant distilled, and mingled in the strongest brown ale, a gallon and a half to a pint. 'Twas extraordinary much sought by the labourers on Sir Bryan's estate. Even more eagerly begged for and carried away was my Palsy and Surfeit Water composed of the juice of poppies, mint, cloves, and coriander seeds, mingled with crushed loafsugar and the best French brandy."

"I guess so!" I said.

"Did you suffer from dropsy, child, or gout," said Lady Deborah, "you would find in that volume the absolute specific."

I said I was afraid I had never had gout, or dropsy either.

"Consumption, then, or sore throat?" said Bryan's ancestress anxiously.

I had had sore throat, and allowed as much.

"For sore throat, an excellent water is made of a peck of snails laid in hyssop, bruised and distilled in new milk," said Lady Deborah, "and drunk fasting. By discreet use of this cordial any sore throat can be cured."

"Why, of course," said I. "The mere thought of the snails would effect the cure. One would get well directly—at least, I should!"

"Then in the treatment of jaundice I have worked absolute wonders, child, with conserve of prepared earthworms, turmeric, and rhubarb, mixed. The complaint flies before it, positively," continued Lady Deborah.

"Or the patient does," I said to myself, but inwardly, remembering the cane.

"You never was bit by a mad dog, was you, chit?" was the astonishing question that came next.

"Good gracious, no!" I exclaimed energetically.

"Because sage, garlic, treacle, and tin filings boiled in a quart of strong mead or clary will serve in this disorder," said Lady Deborah. "You pour it into the party bitten by a quarter of a pint at a time."

"I should never pour it," I said decidedly. "I should be too scared the party would bite *me*, and then there'd be two of us, foaming and acting awful!"

"But supposing you was pitted after a bout of smallpox, and desired to efface the scars," continued Lady Deborah, just as though I had not spoken, "you would find on the hundredth page the worthy Dr. Burgess's recipe for a salve, of oil of tartar, pounded docks and green goose fat, considered infallible." She sighed meditatively.

"Did you—?" I hinted, as delicately as I could.

"The ingredients must be mingled at the time of the new moon, when Venus is in the ascendant, and Jupiter is an evening star. I fear, chit," she sighed, "that my knowledge of astronomics was faulty. So little result I obtained that for a while I was plunged in despair."

"I'm real sorry, dear Lady Deborah!" I said gently.

"But I despaired not long," resumed Bryan's ancestress. "I shut myself in my still-room and kitchen—not to weep and lament, but to work. I had ceased to be the queen of my husband's heart, but I learned to be the goddess of his table. Men are stomach first, child, and heart afterwards. What man would not lose a lover to gain so accomplished a cook as I became?" Her lean, narrow figure dilated, her expanding hoops seemed to fill the room, her keen grey eyes flamed like burning knots of lightwood behind her glasses.

"My fame was sounded throughout the county. 'Lady Deb's battaglio pie,' the bloods toasted now, instead of Lady Deb's skin of cream and roses, and Lady Deb's salmigondin, her patty royal, her cock salmon with buttered lobster, and her tansy fritters, they raved upon, instead of her bright eyes, red lips, pearly teeth, and clustered hair. And I bore it, chit! and curtsied and thanked 'em kindly, though I wished the dishes might surfeit 'em, with all my heart!"

"Oh, poor Lady Deborah!" I said, my heart in my voice.

"I blame them not now!" She lifted her lean hand. "There are no men that love not good eating and drinking—even the saints that denied themselves; and for the women—I'm one of 'em myself, chit, or was—and know whether they sip nectar from blossoms, as they would have the silly men believe, or have at the cold chine and apple-tart in the buttery on the sly, an hour before the dinner-bell."

She fanned herself, and producing from a deep, swinging pocket a thin, black bone rod with a little hand carved at the end, put it to its definite purpose with an energy that made me shiver. William Blake drew the ghost of a flea, I remembered, as Lady Deborah pocketed the little black rod again.

"Please go on, madam . . . You interested me so much about Sir Bryan. Did he reform and become a real devoted husband again?" I asked timidly.

"I tell thee, Lyddy—they call you Lyddy for short, don't they?" resumed Lady Deborah—"he was mine from his shoe-buckle to his wig-tie. He worshipped the tiles of my kitchen—blue-and-white Dutch, and of a pretty fancy. He took glory to himself in the envy of other men; fox-hunting lords and squires, fat-jowled justices of the peace, doctors of divinity, and doctors of law. He never wearied to his dying day of the triumphs of my cookery, especially roasted sucking-pig stuffed with farced chestnuts, and battaglio pie."

"I guess that's good, anyhow!" I said. "It sounds so."

" 'Tis made of young chickens, squab pigeons, quails, partridges and larks," said the ghost of Lady Deborah, drying a shadowy tear. "You truss them, put 'em in your dish lined with rich paste, add sweetbreads, cockscombs, a quart of oysters, sliced sheep's tongues, the marrow of a dozen bones, cloves, mace, nutmegs, the yolks of hard eggs, and forced-meat balls . . . Cover with butter, pour in a pint of cream, and draw the paste over the pie. When done—"

"It's soon done, I guess," said I, for the recital made me feel quite hungry. "My! it must have been rich!"

"That is why I was left a widow, my dear," said the poor old ghost of Lady Deborah, applying the ghost of a lace pocket-handkerchief—darned—to her eyes.

"Through—through a battaglio pie?" I gasped, appalled by the savour of tragedy that rose from the dish.

"Through a battaglio pie. Mr. Pope made use of the incident in his *Moral Essays*," said Lady Deborah, "where 'tis a jowl of salmon and not a pie. Alas, yes! Odious as it sounds, I was the cause of my Bryan's too early end. Year by year he had, thanks to the perfection of my cookery, become more and more addicted to the pleasures of the table. Racing, gaming, hunting, had become in his eyes the mere means to gain the appetite for fresh enjoyment. His fine complexion had become a dusky red, his chiselled features swelled, his eyes retired behind cushions of fat, his waist vanished, and three chins depended upon his laced cravat."

"Oh!" I cried in horror.

"He drank hugely, but his drinking was moderate in proportion to his eating," said Sir Bryan's widow. "Too well I remember the odious event . . . 'Twas his name-day; he had five boon companions join him at the table, I put forth all my powers fitly to celebrate the anniversary. There could not be a prettier supper than that my husband sat to—not if I was to die this minute—I crave pardon, dear Lydia, for forgetting that I am dead! The first course was roasted pike and smelts—being June, pike was in season. Westphalia ham and young fowls, marrow puddings, haunch of venison roasted, ragout of lamb, sweetbreads, *fricassée* of young rabbits, umbles, a dish of mullets, roasted ducks, and custards."

"And six men sat down to a supper like that?" I said, feeling my eyes opening to their widest extent.

"Nay, child, that was only the first course," said Lady Deborah, sniffing at her silver pomander. "The second course was a dish of young pheasants, a dish of soles and eels, a potato-salad, a jowl of sturgeon, a dish of tarts and cheese-cakes, a rock of snow with syllabubs, *and* that fatal, that ever-to-be-regretted battaglio pie!" She wiped her eyes and fanned herself. " 'Twas the crown of the banquet . . . Sir Bryan and his guests called for a fresh magnum of claret when it appeared . . . 'Gentlemen and boon companions,' said he, with the drops of perspiration standing on his purple forehead, and his wig pushed back—I can see it now, for I was peeping through the old buttery dish-slide the servants scarce ever used—'Gentlemen, here's another bumper to the health of Lady Deborah Corbryan, the best wife and the best cook in the Four Kingdoms!' And the gentlemen tossed down the wine, child, but they were full to the throats. Justice Sir Barnwell Plumptree and Sir George Cockerell (for he and Bryan became great friends in later years), Nainby Friswell and Mr. Selwyn, and Colonel Sir Harry Firebrace of the King's Dragoons. They could only look and water at the chops as my dear Sir Bryan cut into the battaglio pie. He cleared a platter full and wiped up the gravy with crust. 'Do ye check?' says he in scorn of the others. 'Do ye balk at the best dish in Christendom? I've supped already, but I wager ye a guinea to a tester all round that I finish the dish!' They took the bet, child, and Sir Bryan put ladle to dish. The ladle dropped with a clatter . . . a surge of blackish purple rose from his chins to his crown . . . 'Death and fire!' says he, 'you've won your money!' and fell, and never uttered word again until he had been blooded by three chirurgeons one after the other, and had had the actual cautery applied. Oh, my dear! Then he came to himself, and 'Is that thou, Deb?' says he. 'I always loved thee, lass! Tell me the truth now, do I live or die?' And the doctor shook his head. 'No hope?' says Sir Bryan. 'Why, then, I'll e'en die as I have lived. Bring me the dish here—I'll e'en finish the rest o' the battaglio pie and turn the tables on Plumptree and the others.' And he did, child—he did. And I lived to wear out my weeds and con over my cookery book but a dozen years after him, and now I'm dead"—the poor lady sobbed —"I do it still, chit—I do it still! My hapless spirit is bound up in the yellow pages of that cookery book. I know not when my bondage shall cease, and rest be mine at last!"

"Poor lady—unhappy ghost!" I cried. "Will nothing bring you peace?"

You would have known you had been interviewing a ghost by the fading outlines of Lady Deborah's form and features, and the way in which the black oak chair upholstered with old gilt leather showed through the hooped skirts of green and pink brocade. Her vanishing lips framed but two other words. . .

"Battaglio pie," she said, and was gone in an instant; and with a crash the cookery book fell to the floor, and I sat up, wondering whether I had been dreaming? On the whole, I guessed I had not. When I picked up the prostrate cookery book, I knew I had not, for one of the many-times dogs'-eared pages was doubled over in a perfectly fresh place, *and the page bore the famous recipe for battaglio pie.*

The post that followed brought my promised letter. The next day brought a marconigram from Bryan. Marconi is hardly the language of love, but it did at a pinch. Parpa was no worse, it said, and I was not to be anxious. Indeed, by the time the liner picked up her pilot off Sandy Hook, the bulletins were so favourable that Bryan decided to return right away, Parpa being quite out of danger. He did return—one of our great Atlantic ferryboats being on the point of starting—and I marconied a message which hit the ship 1,065 miles west of the Lizard, to say I was well and happy, and learning to cook!

That was so. I had respectfully replaced Lady Deborah's cookery book upon her *escritoire*, after copying the fatal and famous recipe for battaglio pie . . . I had made friends with the ruler of the Abbey kitchen, and under her tuition was rapidly mastering the secret of flaky pastry.

June was scarcely over our heads; all the ingredients were procurable, though the heavy groan that burst from the head gamekeeper's bosom, when I demanded three young partridges, I never shall forget. He brought them, though, and I had but to amass the quail, the squab pigeon, the cockscombs, sweetbreads, oysters, sheep's tongues, and so forth, from other sources. Thus on the afternoon previous to Bryan's return, I lined a stately dish with rich pie-paste, I piled in all the good things, added the eggs, forcemeat, spices, cream and butter, and drew the cover over all, ornamenting it with devices cut with antique pewter moulds that Lady Deborah herself may have used. I glazed the outside with egg-white. And then I saw the pie slide into a gentle oven, and knew my task would soon be done. An hour later, as I lay resting in my favourite corner of the spindle-legged, tapestry-covered sofa in the long drawing-room, I had a second visit from Lady Deborah. She wore her black silk calash this time, and behind her great silver-rimmed spectacles her eyes snapped and sparkled with a joy that was—was it malign? She spread out her rustling brocade skirts as I rose up, and responded to my hesitating curtsey with the grandest cheese I had ever seen.

"I am vastly obleeged, Lydia," she said, smiling her old cheeks into creases. "You have behaved monstrous genteelly, child, and I feel that I shall owe my freedom to your generosity. I have taken measures that the reputation of the Abbey shall not suffer, as there is a lamentable lack of *ton* about a family residence without a ghost. Sir Umphrey, who got grant of the demesne from King Henry VIII, and, as you may have heard, murdered the abbot who took exception to the grant, has arranged to haunt the inhabited wings as well as the shut-up portion. You have also a third share in a banshee brought into the family by one of the Desmonds, who intermarried with us in 1606, and there is a hugely impressive death-watch in the wainscoting of your room. Therefore, I need have no scruples in taking the change of air so necessary for vapours."

She took her great calash and spreading brocades away. I forgot her—forgot the pie—forgot everything an hour later, in the joy of Bryan's arrival. With the aid of the housekeeper and by the advice of the cook, I had had prepared a real traveller's dinner, and at last my battaglio pie was placed upon the table before the master of the house.

Such a pie! a mountain of golden flaky crust, exhaling delicious, tempting, savoury odours. I looked across it at Bryan, and laughed in sheer delight at his astonishment.

"So this is the joke you have been keeping to yourself all the evening, Lydia, you little witch!" said Bryan, laughing too. "A pie—a monster pie—and a savoury pie, too, made by your own hands, what?" He sniffed the delicious steam with expanded nostrils and filled his glass with Port. "Here's to the health of Lady Lydia Corbryan," he cried gaily, "the best wife and the best cook in the Four Kingdoms—not to mention the Realms beyond the Seas!"

Where had I heard those words—most of them—before? I grew dizzy as Bryan seized the silver pastry-knife and spoon and plunged into the depths of the battaglio pie . . . A change seemed to have come over him, the outlines of his face and figure seemed to waver and alter as I gazed speechlessly, waiting for something to come . . .

"I've dined already," my husband cried in a thick voice that frightened me, "but I'll bet you a sovereign to a sixpence that I finish the dish!"

"Bryan!" I screamed. "Bryan!" and barely recognised him to whom I appealed. That crimson face, with the moist shine of perspiration glossing it, the powdered wig pushed back from the swollen forehead, the piggish, twinkling eyes, gross, flabby mouth, and three chins dropping over the flowing lace cravat . . . Strange to me . . . all strange, yet so horribly, horribly, familiar! I must have risen from my chair and rushed to him, for I found myself clinging to a man's arm and crying, "Don't touch it! If you love me, Bryan, don't touch it!" over and over again.

"Of course not, if you don't wish it, little woman!" said the dear familiar voice. Bryan was holding me, and the face I loved was pressed comfortingly to mine. "Look here, Pet, I didn't mean to vex you. I'll throw it out of the window if you want me to."

"Y-yes!" I sobbed, with chattering teeth. "Th-throw it out . . . do, please!" and Bryan heaved up the huge pie-dish in his muscular hands.

"Open the window, please," he said, and I hurried to obey. The casement swung wide upon a square of star-jewelled darkness . . . Did I hear a shrill, thin, eerie scream? Did I hear another casement crash open, somewhere in the west wing, as the battaglio pie was hurled into the night?

I asked Phee next morning to accompany me to Lady Deborah's room. The intrepid girl followed, only delaying to wind a thread of red marking-cotton nine times round her left thumb, and tuck her Aunt Dinah's hymnbook into what she termed "de bosom" of her gown. As I climbed the stairs, threaded recollected passages, and with just a little qualm of nervousness opened the not-to-be-forgotten door, a blast of cold air saluted me. The casement swung open, fragments of its shattered panes still jagging in the leads, and a yellowish snow of torn papers littered the floor. They were fragments of the cookery book, torn to atoms by a force unknown . . . What force? The portrait of Lady Deborah gazed stonily from over the fireplace and made no answer.

What would have happened had Bryan indulged the hereditary instinct that led him to hunger, even after a full meal, for battaglio pie? Would he have ended existence like the unlucky glutton, his ancestor, in stertorous coma, unrelieved by depletion? Should I have died of grief, and haunted the Abbey in Lady Deborah's stead, a disconsolate, widowed shade, continually brooding over a battered edition of *The Compleat Housewife*? Who can say?

But it smelt wonderfully good. There have been hungry moments when I have half regretted not tasting it, the sole achievement in the cookery line I am destined ever to accomplish.

I have never seen Lady Deborah since!

(*The recipes quoted by the ghost of Lady Deborah have been taken from a copy of* THE COMPLEAT HOUSEWIFE *in the author's possession, dated 1733.*)

The Mother of Turquoise

A Story of the Mines of Hathor

I.

I have just finished reading Professor Flanders's book, *My Expedition from Suez through the Sinaitic Peninsula.*

To the Professor I accorded respect. To the memory of my dead friend Majendie, that swelling of the heart, that dimness of the eyes, which, in a woman would herald the sure relief of tears.

The Professor is absolutely correct in recording that many of the finest of the wonderful mountain-inscriptions at Rekhareh have been broken and defaced. Wantonly bashed into pieces by a hammer—the perpetrators of this act of brutal ignorance being "certain English adventurers searching for deposits of turquoise under a concession from the Egyptian Government, now mercifully annulled."

Quite correct, Professor. The bashing was done under my personal superintendence by half a dozen brawny Arab workmen, animated by the distant hope of *bakshish* and the present stimulant of leathery-tasting water, warm out of the camel-bags, and sprinkled with millet-meal.

Were it necessary to commit the wanton act over again, I would do so, despite the shriek of the Egyptologist, showing due respect to the nobly-sculptured image of King Ketrah of the First Dynasty, whose reign dates back to 5291 B.C. There was no devilry in the few lines of hieroglyphics recording His Majesty's victory over the twin rebel chieftains of the Bedawy, represented as crouching in halters before their conqueror. But Firân and Abou Musa and their relations were warm to the work, and spoiled the fine bas-reliefs before I could prevent it.

Three years before the War, I answered an advertisement, and interviewed the Directors of the Sinaitic Turquoise Syndicate, Limited, at their offices in Bowchurch Street, City. They wanted a mining engineer with qualifications as an assayer and no objection to a hot climate, and I wanted a shop—out of England for choice. To tell the truth, there was a woman at the bottom of my desire to get quit, for some years at all events, of my native land. The Head-Director of the Turquoise Syndicate was a smug, white-faced, chop-whiskered man in a glossy, tightly-buttoned frock-coat and elaborately-creased trousers, who, when I had signed on as engineer and assayer to the Expedition at fifteen pounds a month, rations, camels, and travelling expenses found, laid himself out to a great extent in moral and religious counsel, and I can see his face now as he held forth to me about Syria being full of temptations for young men with unbridled animal passions and no religious principles. He quoted the Israelites, of whom there fell three and twenty thousand in one day; and promised to put up prayers for the guidance and protection of the Expedition. I saw my fat-faced friend's name by accident in a police-court case, a year later, and agreed that he knew something about temptations. As to the prayers, he wanted them all for himself, I judge, going by the things that happened at Rekharet.

I suppose the scrapping with Turkey about Akabah induced the pre-War reader to rub up his geographical knowledge of that naked, scorching tongue of barren desert and naked mountain, known as the Sinaitic Peninsula. The ancient Egyptians worked turquoise mines in the Wady Maghara when the Great Pyramid was building under the lash of Menkaura. The Bedawy knew of the mines in Wady Rekharet, but they kept the secret as only Arabs can, until the Nineteenth Dynasty saw the departure of the Hebrews from Egypt, and the pent-up waters of the Bitter Lakes swept down from the north-west upon the hosts of Menepthah, the Pharaoh of the Exodus. Thenceforward the glory of Egypt reached its climax and began its decline.

At least, so Majendie told me one day on the journey out, and he gave one the feeling of being a man who knew. Majendie and I were the Expedition, not counting my fox-terrier Vic, and the Arabs and camels we chartered at Suez.

Majendie was a well-knit, broad-shouldered, keen-eyed fellow of twenty-five or six, quiet, well-bred, and full of knowledge and information. The son of a well-known consulting-physician with a handle to his name, Majendie had incurred the paternal indignation for betaking himself, after securing at the age of twenty-four, his degree as Doctor of Medicine at University College, to fields of research particularly his own. In physiology and experimental chemistry he won distinction, and having a fine talent for the acquirement of living languages (he had French, German, Spanish, Modern Greek, Hindustani, and Arabic at his tongue's end) young Arthur began, much to the disgust of the distinguished consulting-physician in Brooker Street, to ferret at the roots of dead tongues. He spent months at the British Museum in the study of Egyptian hieroglyphic and Babylonian cuneiform inscriptions, and ended by accepting the berth of surgeon on the steamship *Delta*, a vessel employed by the Government of Egypt for lighthouse service in the Red Sea.

"In the intervals of Krooboy colics and Arab eye-diseases, I managed to make some expeditions into the Hedjaz and the Arabian Desert," he told me, "but just as things were getting interesting came the tug of duty at the other end. Now our friends in Bowchurch Street, if not liberal where cash is concerned, are generous as regards time. When we leave Suez and head our camels south for the historical three days' journey into the wilderness, we are at liberty to be lost for six months, so long as we turn up at the other end of the time—"

"With plenty of turquoises," I chimed in.

"The real article," said Majendie. "Half the so-called turquoises on the London, Cairo, and Jaffa markets are odontolite, fossil bone of mammoth or dinotherium impregnated with phosphate of iron. The bony structure may be detected under the microscope by anybody who cares to look; but I have a belief that people are fond of being swindled."

He lifted his brown, well-shaped left hand to flip the ash from his cigar, and I caught a blue gleam from a splendid stone in a rough native-worked setting of yellow gold worn upon the little finger.

"At any rate," said I, "you got your money's worth when you bought that seal." For the turquoise was the size of a large hazel-nut with a segment sheared off one side. The setting was curious: three eagle-claws, nipping the stone tightly, so that while its rounded part was next the hand, its flattened surface was exposed to view.

"This intaglio? . . . I did not buy it," said Majendie, quietly glancing at the ring and then at me, in a baffling sort of way. "Nor was it given me," he added, in the same tone—then added, "I found it—with several others—where I hope to find some more by and by, luck being with us." And his expression showed how keen he was on the Expedition turning out a success.

We sat on a couple of long Indian cane chairs on a verandah overlooking the freshly-watered courtyard of the hotel at Suez. The dragoman who had bargained to furnish us with dromedaries, drivers, a cook, and a guide had just made his salaam and departed, and we were waiting for my "*brudah*", who had undertaken through his fraternal rogue to purvey our supplies. It flashed on me then that instead of merely being an employé of the Turquoise Syndicate, engaged to travel to a given centre and prospect for the gem desired, Majendie was the originator of the Expedition and the sole proprietor of the secret of our destination. I taxed him with this upon the spot, and he owned up that an Arab stoker on board the *Delta* whom he had cured of eye-worm, or *filaria*—one of the many horrible diseases mainly due to the habitual drinking of bad water—had "put him on to something". More he would not say. But he struck me as being more quietly exultant and less excited than a man would be who was striking out in an unknown direction towards the attainment of an uncertain end.

We squared matters with the dragoman and his "*brudah*" in about three days, and started with quite an imposing string of mules, dromedaries, baggage-camels, and Arabs. It was mid-June, and the scorching pebbly slopes, the stunted tamarisks and acacias, the baked and splitting rocks, and dried-up watercourses endlessly succeeding made up a cheerless panorama which would have depressed me, had Majendie proved a less pleasant travelling companion. But in three days' time, when we reached the first oasis of Wady Gharandel, and then made straight for the mountains, I was ready to be cheerful on my own account. The elastic desert air, the boundless sky, the wonderful colour of the rocks, blue, green, black, crimson, lilac, golden, pink, and white, the soaring brown and white eagles of the heights, the silver-grey rock-falcons and the rock-pigeons, red-legged partridge, and other game that occasionally fell to my gun reconciled me to Syria, its scorpions, beetles, and plague of flies. We passed Wady Magarah, where the first tablets of hieroglyphics are found, and then, bearing to the left, came upon the Written Valley.

Other travellers have devoted pages to that wonderful spot. I am not good at descriptions. Briefly, then, let me say that for four miles our caravans defiled through a lofty gorge of red granite, the smoothed surfaces of whose rocks are literally covered with irregularly-carved inscriptions, some larger, others smaller, in characters measuring from a foot high to half an inch. High up upon the towering face of the precipice rising left and right I could distinguish others, and almost every large boulder at our feet bore similar records, less deeply cut, in some instances scratched on the stone.

"Who did them? What are they? Historical records or votive tablets, or prayer—or what?" I sang out, shutting up my Dollery binoculars after a long satisfying stare, and addressing the back of Majendie's solar topee.

Majendie looked back over his shoulder as we slowly forged along in single file, narrowing his eyes in the dazzling, blinding sun-flood that came tumbling on our heads from between the double ranges of fantastic limestone peaks above.

"If anybody knew for certain, old man, there wouldn't be much good in our being where we are," he said, with a dash of triumph in his tone. "When the old Coptic monks built the Convent of Mount Sinai this character of hieroglyphic was unknown, and since a Teutonic wiseacre, Beer of Leipzic, published a so-called key to it at Paris in 1840 nobody has managed to decipher them. Lepsius calls them the work of the Shepherd Kings, Layard never saw them, Dr. Flanders means to come here one day . . .

But he has not got here yet," said Majendie, jerking at his dromedary's heavy single rein. And as the desert ships began to pitch fore and aft in preparation for kneeling: "And we have," he added in that oddly exultant tone. "*Ai'iwa Musa*, we camp here . . . This is our journey's end, Randolph."

We pitched no tent that night, but had our carpets spread and our wooden native bedsteads set up in a roomy curve that yawned in the face of the red granite precipice. The Arabs lighted fires, and when the splendid Syrian moon rose and looked down into the gorge we were supping on kabobbed mutton, tomatoes, and macaroni, and feeling— at least I was—like a band of brigands in an opera. After supper Majendie and I smoked and chatted, and he told me that in the streaks of red marl running in the faults and cleavages of the granite and in the veins of matrix permeating the red sandstone, as in scattered nodules of the same, knocked from the precipices by mountain torrents or struck by lightning from their face, the jewels we were searching for would be found. True rock turquoises, susceptible of receiving a brilliant polish, and reflecting light from under the surface.

"Like that stone in your ring," I said, pointing to it with the stem of my briar-root pipe. For the peculiar property possessed by Majendie's stone of seeming to give out radiance and colour, had never struck me so forcibly as at that moment. In the combined light of the blazing dry-wood fire and the flare of an Arab torch of rags dipped in resin, and held on the end of a cleft stick stuck into a crevice in the rock-wall, the turquoise seemed to burn with an azure flame. And as Majendie drew off the ring and put it in my hand—a thing he had never done before—he said a thing I remembered afterwards:

"The stone of the goddess remembers its ancient home. The Child of Hathor knows she is near her Mother, whose shrine and temple are here, in the heart of the granite hills."

I held the gleaming stone up where the mingled lights drew out its fullest beauty. Cut upon the level face of the turquoise, was the profile figure of a woman, naked save for a girdle, and crowned with a crescent, holding a serpent in one hand and in the other a lotus-flower. Majendie had probably found the ring somewhere near, possibly in the temple of which he spoke. But I gave it back without question.

That night, lying on my native bedstead of bamboo and native webbing, with a valise under my head and a rug over me, I had a queer dream. It seemed in my dream that a shining figure stood in the entrance of our cave, which glowed with radiant light that streamed from her crescent-shaped coronal. Facing us full, she stretched towards me a lotus-flower and towards my sleeping companion a writhing snake. And my blood was chilled by the look of malice in her brilliant eyes, blue and hard as turquoises beneath black bow-like, joined eyebrows, and by the mockery that smiled upon her scarlet lips. And cold to the very heart, and with an indescribable sensation of suffocation, I awakened.

The valley outside the cave we slept in was flooded with dazzling white moonlight, the sleeping camels, the tethered mules, the Arabs under their improvised shelters of felt or blankets, or garments laid across sticks, the strangely-shaped boulders and dwarfed trees, showed as distinctly as by day. Beside me, a few feet away, Majendie breathed heavily. Indifferently I glanced towards him, realised the dreadful meaning of the slender, semi-upright Thing that swayed above the sleeper's broad heaving chest, and then—rousing my torpid energies with a desperate effort—I softly reached down, picked up a loaded stick that lay beside me, and with a long arm and a well-directed swipe, sent the snake flying.

"What is it?" shouted Majendie, waking up.

"Only a puff-adder on your chest, that's all!" I had got my gun by this time and was thoroughly awake. "There he goes over that patch of sand between those tamarisk-bushes."

Sitting on the bottom of my bed I took aim as I spoke, meaning to riddle him with a dose of shot.

"Stop!" Majendie shouted. He leaped from his own *ankareb* and gripped my arm. "Don't kill it. Confound you, man! you'll ruin everything! Why didn't you let the snake alone?"

He was ghastly pale, or else it was the moonlight, and the hand that gripped me burned—I felt it through the sleeve of my flannel shirt as I lowered the gun.

"Why—the damned thing would have bitten you!" I protested.

"It was a message—can't you see? A message!" persisted Majendie, shaking.

Convinced that he had got a touch of fever, I offered him quinine and Eno. He declined both, but judging by his haggard looks in the morning, he slept no more that night. Worrying about the intercepted message, no doubt. The message! Why a sane man should suppose a snake—deadly poisonous at that—would come crawling to his bed in the middle of the night to give him a message, I couldn't imagine. It was easier to say to myself that too much swotting over Egyptian hieroglyphics had made Majendie cranky, that, in fact, though a pleasant man to associate with, he had a tile off, and so on.

We unpacked the picks and crowbars, grappling-irons and wired ropes we had brought along, also the box of dynamite blasting cartridges we had with discretion tied

112

to the back of the quietest mule. Our Arabs had found a spring of good water in a cave marked out by the fresh verdure growing about its base, and the sheikh of a tribal family of Bedawy found us out and sent a messenger with a present of *dhurra* cakes, to ask if we wanted to hire labourers. From him Majendie learned that the gorge was locally called Wady Rekharet. The sheikh added, with great certainty, that no turquoises had ever been found there within the memory of man. Majendie laughed harshly as he translated to me the Bedawin's utterance.

"Man is such a short-lived kind of animal, with such an uncommonly feeble memory," he jeered, "one can't rely much upon him. Unless he writes his records in the imperishable rock, and makes that his witness which Time itself cannot destroy, as these Egypto-Semitic miners did who kept their ledgers there!" He pointed to a row of inscriptions baking in the noonday glare on the precipice high above, and began to reel off in English:

"Therefore we bless thee, fecund Hathor, the blue-eyed Mother of the Jewel of the Rocks, that thou hast been favourable unto us, Khita the Syrian, Gad the Phoenician, and Tani-hat the Egyptian, sent hither by Menepthah the King, the conqueror beloved of Amen, Pthah and Harmachis, we, duly making oblation of incense and burnt sacrifice—"

"Of a kid," I put in, vaguely reminded of Scriptural passages I had heard droned out on Sundays by our good old vicar at home.

"Of a kid—that's just it," said Majendie with an awkward-sounding laugh, "and some time or other I'll show you the temple where they offered it."

He turned to the Bedawy chief then, whose name was Erbkam, and began bargaining away at a great rate for able-bodied workmen with pickaxes and *maktafs*, the shallow baskets the Arabs carry dirt and tailings in. The

Bedawy were encamped a mile farther up the gorge, and when the last haggle about the rate of pay had ended in an arrangement for two piastres a day, their bread and *dhurra*-water to be brought by the women, we accompanied Erbkam to the camp.

There was nothing to be seen but a group of villainously dirty felt tents, some hobbled camels diligently eating nothing off the bare boulders, a starved mule or two, a ribby horse, a gang of sore-eyed children, and some prematurely aged women. Then out of a tent came a pretty young creature with gazelle-eyes and a gold coin among the silver ones in her black hair, leading a frail little figure bowed into a hoop and covered with a mass of rags. This was Erbkam's great-grandmother, a lady of ancient family, celebrated through the whole peninsula as a prophetess, the sheikh explained through Majendie.

"Certainly, if rags and dirt and old age make a prophetess, she ought to be one," I said to Majendie. "The young lady, now, is more in my line," and I lifted my hat in my best style to the owner of the gazelle-eyes and the gold coin. I could swear she blushed, a manifestation of shyness as unusual with the Arab as with the camel; and I learned that her name was Aissa. The prophetess, who was blind, was called Thorah. Whether she was blind really I never knew. Only where eyes should have been were folds of wrinkles, shaded by the ragged fringe of her headcloth, and being toothless and palsied as well, she moved and chattered like a rock-monkey. Not that she could not get over the ground easily enough: daily she accompanied the pretty Aissa, who was the chief's daughter by his youngest wife, down to our camp with the women who brought bread, and I have seen her standing on a boulder near where some of our workmen were quarrying, mowing and mopping and pointing her stick as if in derision at our futile attempts to strike the turquoise vein.

For day by day the "blue jewel of Hathor" eluded us. Neither in the red marl or the limestone did we come upon a trace. There was plenty of copper ore, genuine and bastard, but we were not in search of copper, and three months had gone over our heads; it was August, and sandstorms harassed us terribly. The spring we had relied on showed signs of drying up, and many of the tins of Chicago meat supplied by the Suez contractor proved, when opened, to contain nothing that a self-respecting carrion-crow could eat. We gave the contents of them decent burial, and lived on *dhurra*-bread, fried bacon, and jam, washed down with coffee. In turns Majendie and I superintended the quarrying-gang and the very primitive crushing-machine we had set up on a plateau of smooth rock. And, I am grateful to say, I learned sufficient Arabic to understand, and to make myself understood. So weeks went by, and the turquoise vein eluded us. Though on either hand of us the living rock testified to the riches the ancient miners had wrung from the place.

"*Mistress of Mafkat*"—Mafkat means the copper country—"*great are thy gifts*", ran the inscription on another tablet Majendie translated, and which I copied down in my notebook. *"For of copper three hundred ingots, one camel's load; and of the turquoise of the rock three baskets and half-a-basket we have received of thy favour, duly making oblation and sacrifice in thy Temple of Dreams."*

"Why did they call it the Temple of Dreams?" I asked.

"Because, after making oblation and sacrifice, they slept in the precincts of the sacred place," returned Majendie, "and in dreams they were shown where the veins of ore and jewel-matrix were to be found."

"Look here!" I said, knocking out the dottle of my pipe and getting up from the boulder I had been sitting on. "I want to see that temple now."

"You don't mind a stiff climb?" Majendie asked. I shook my head, filling my pipe anew, and we set out, with a flap of bread and a bottle of water, it being Saturday afternoon.

A three-mile tramp up the Written Valley brought us to the place, copper ores liberally outcropping in the rock, and huge mounds of black slag marking the smelting-places of the ancient miners. The ruins of the temple were perched on a platform of pinkish sandstone jutting out from the face of the precipice about a hundred feet above our heads. Square bevelled holes in the rock-face showed where the wooden steps of a kind of ladder had once been fixed, and beside them dangled a hide rope, securely fastened, as we found by hauling on it, to a stone or beam above.

It was a stiff climb, but the place was worth it. The front elevation of the temple had been carved out of the solid pink sandstone, and the great central chamber went back into the heart of the mountain, whence it had been hollowed for sixty feet or more. There were altars of the shape one sees upon Egyptian temple friezes, great beds of wood-ashes, layers nearly petrified and others comparatively fresh, the fuel for which must have been brought from great distances, a variety of tanks and basins for ceremonial washing—one wondered where they had obtained the water to fill them— and, round the central chamber, a honeycomb of cells, each furnished with a stone bench for the sleeper, a stone pillow for his head, a quantity of lively black nipper-tail beetles, and one or more active scorpions.

"You see, the walls are covered with inscriptions of thanks, and each of the pillars is a memorial of some lucky find," said Majendie. "When I was here two years ago—"

"I knew you had been here before," I said, sucking my finger, which I had barked rather badly during the ascent, "although your not knowing the real name of the Wady puzzled me."

"Every wandering desert tribe have their own names for places," said Majendie, "and on the return journey the names are changed as often as not. Historical and geographical purists may suffer; but you can't whack into an Arab's head that a hill is a hill when he is coming down it. See, there is the image of the Mother of Turquoise herself, above the middle altar. Don't go too near!"

"Why not?" I queried, staring at Majendie. "You don't hold that there's any sanctity about the place, do you?"

Then, as he turned away, I went off to the altar, for the likeness of the profile figure carved on a great rock tablet above, to the figure cut on the turquoise on Majendie's ring strangely attracted me. There was the crescent-shaped headdress, and in the outstretched hands of the figure were the lotus-bud and the snake. The altar was broken, but a deep channel to carry off the blood of the sacrifice ran round it, and there were little culverts at the corners. And a long-shaped bundle, apparently of stained and weather-beaten native cloth, lay across the stone at the feet of the inscrutable smiling statue. I could not imagine what the bundle might contain, until, stretching my arm over the edge of the altar, I had touched it lightly with my finger. Then I pulled back my hand (the damaged one) quickly enough, as I shouted to Majendie:

"Why, here is the mummy of a child!"

Majendie made an incoherent sound in answer, and I took another observation of the poor little corpse. The dry desert air had withered and desiccated it until it must have been as light as a roll of palm-fibre. The withered little monkey-hands were folded on the breast, the feet crossed together. What had induced its parents to bury it there I was at a loss to conceive. Then a dark series of stains upon the altar-stone running to the channel chiselled at the edges enlightened me to the hideous truth. When, I could

117

not guess; but it flashed upon me that at some not very distant time that native child had been offered up to the goddess-demon of the sandstone temple. Now I knew the kind of sacrifice with which those ancient miners, Khita the Syrian, Gad the Phoenician, Tani-hat and Co., had rewarded the lady of the horned headdress. And I did not admire the lady. But unwittingly I had paid her tribute in the fluid she preferred, for a drop or two of fresh blood from my torn finger was soaking into the dry surface of the sandstone altar.

"Come away, come away!" cried Majendie, angrily, as I began to express my opinion of Egypto-Semitic deities. "I was a fool to bring you here. Shut up and come away!"

II.

We scrambled down by the hide rope which was made fast with a very workmanlike turn and clove-hitch, to one of the memorial pillars, and tramped back over the scorching boulders to our camp.

Next day, from a nodule of sandstone, one of our workmen chipped out the first turquoise. A little later I found one myself, a fine and perfect stone. Two others were found, and then the fog of bad luck settled down upon us again. The Arabs chipped and picked and crushed—the supplies got scarcer, and Majendie took to disappearing for hours every day. When he came back he would explain that he had been yarning with the sheikh. And being slightly smitten in that direction myself, I suspected him of carrying on a flirtation with Aissa, and taxed the wearer of the gold coin with giddiness next time she came down to the camp, in the broken Arabic which she herself had taught me.

Aissa shook her head and looked at me out of the corners of her gazelle eyes.

118

"Aissa say no, she is no fountain for the Angleezi lord to drink at, nor palm-tree to cover him from the sun." She shook her head again energetically. "And if you want to know with whom the Angleezi make sweet talk, it is Thorah. Thorah always."

Thorah, the blind prophetess, great-grandmother to Erbkam the sheikh. The notion of Majendie making love to the old lady and braving in the violence of his infatuation the swords, rusty spears, and wool-tufted, muzzle-loading guns of her descendants, tickled me to laughter. But Aissa looked grave.

"Thorah nothing to joke about, great magic-woman," she said. I know that "*es sehr*" meant magic of the black or evil description, and certainly the old woman had a witch-like look. I made my peace with the gazelle-eyed maiden, treating her to brown sugar from the camp store-box, a delicacy in which she revelled. And I was racking my brains to find a reason for Majendie's suddenly developed preference for the society of the sorceress when he returned, very haggard and nervous and with a bandaged arm, and ordered the Arabs to strike their quarrying operations and transfer themselves, their baskets, and their tools to a new spot on the opposite side of the valley, about a quarter of a mile below our camp. Then he went away again, and did not reappear until the gold and crimson sunrise rolled down from peak to peak of the solemn mountains and the blue shadows of night fled back to the caves.

That day we struck a rich vein of splendid size and quality. The bottom of the cotton-wool-lined tin box that held our finds began to be covered, and the prospects of the Turquoise Syndicate looked up day by day. We stored away a rich collection of pieces of matrix on our own account, that being our perquisite, before Fortune deserted us again. The vein became unfruitful—suddenly ceased. The Arabs idled and smoked, convinced that until the Djinn who had bewitched their tools relented, business would remain at a standstill. And Majendie took to straying again by day, and groaning and talking in his sleep of nights. One night, when he was more hag-ridden and voluble than usual, I'll own I sat up and listened, as he argued with somebody who wanted him to give in and do, once, just once more— something that would bring untold wealth to all of us. He held out against the invisible persuader until the sweat rolled down his livid, working face—shown as plainly as by day in the white moonlight that poured into our sleeping-cave. Thoughts of a girl in England—you see there was one in *his* case too!—seemed to hold him back from doing what must stain his honour and imperil his soul in the effort to gain riches for her, and earn him her loathing instead of her love, if ever she should come to know it.

"What matters the girl? Thou shalt drink of the cup that kings have coveted, and taste the joy of joys!"

The voice was not Majendie's, but a woman's, of wonderful sonority and sweetness. It came from nowhere, woke the sleeping echoes in the rock-hollows with its utterance and then ceased. And the pronunciation of the Arabic words was not what I had learned from Aissa. A foreigner who should painstakingly acquire English from a London flower-girl, and then hear it spoken by the greatest of all English-speaking actresses, might have found the same difference as I did. Next morning I woke to find Majendie gone, and an hour afterwards two Arab women came down from the camp above, looking for the sheikh's youngest child.

"At dawn we saw the child Zelim outside his mother's tent playing with a jerboa Aissa tamed and gave him. Perhaps it strayed and Zelim followed. The girl Aissa sobs and weeps, for this is an evil place for babes to stray in, as other tribes have learned, *Ahi! Awalis!*"

They uttered shrill cries, shutting their mouths with their joined fingers so as to produce a vibrating sound. The howl was exactly like the *whillelu* of Irishwomen at a wake. They should never see the child again, they said; he had been snatched away by Djinnis, as his elder brother had been, two years ago, in that very place.

"Why not search for him in the caves?" I asked. And then an idea struck me, and I questioned: "Was the kiddy adventurous enough to have strayed higher up the Valley of Writings, and sufficiently active to have climbed up where the camel's-hide rope hung down from the mouth of the holy place above?"

I designated the Temple of Hathor by the Arabic word for shrine, because I did not know how otherwise to express myself. The women clapped their hands and shrieked in horror. *That* a holy place, forsooth! Why, it was the home of every devil, literally speaking, in the peninsula. Not a man, woman, or child of the Araba would set foot in the accursed place, and so on.

And yet my thoughts ran continually on the pink temple in the sandstone cliff where the two-years-old mummy, of what I guessed to be the child Zelim's elder brother, lay under the image of Hathor, the Mother of Turquoise. And as I drew lines with my stick in the red-hot gravel, and watched the ants running in and out of them, I wondered if the accidental spilling of the blood from my torn finger on that channelled stone had had anything to do with our first find of turquoise, and also, whether Majendie's bandaged arm had had anything to do with later discoveries? And then—with a horrible leap and sinking of the heart, the new link of evidence joined to the old, and I saw a motive in the abduction of the child Zelim.

"Horrible! Impossible!" I muttered to myself. But suspicion had fixed her fangs in me. I made an excuse that saved me from breaking bread with Majendie that night. He loomed hideous in the new light that had broken in upon me. I remembered that double play on words about "the kid", the dream I had had, and the awakening. I recalled how Majendie had forbidden me to shoot the snake—the reptile he had treated as a messenger—and his chagrin and vexation at my discovery of the mummied corpse of the native child in the bundle that lay upon the altar of Hathor in the pink temple. Why had he taken me there?

Was he in the habit of going to the place? Next time he left the camp I would follow him—"peeled", as the Americans say—with my dagger-knife and revolver.

He did not go to bed that night, but sat in the moonlight by the remains of our camp fire, with his eyes fixed on the glowing embers. He had grown haggard, was terribly changed, in the last few months. I could see him from where I lay, and then my eyes closed against my will—I was dozing when a long wailing cry came down the Wady from the Arab camp. I woke up. I saw that Majendie no longer sat by the fire, whose ashes lay dead. And I rose up and slipped on a pair of rubber-soled cricketing shoes, and set out, up the shadowed side of the Written Valley, walking with long, noiseless strides in the direction of the Arab camp. The wailing had come from there; a funeral dance was in full swing as I slunk past. Evidently the lost boy was figuratively being interred with honours.

Poor little devil! What had happened to him? What was that odd, humped-up figure fifty yards ahead of me, getting over the moon-bleached rocks and boulders with the agility of a frightened spider? I quickened my pace to gain a nearer view. It was the prophetess, Thorah. Blind or not, the way in which that old bundle of rags got over the ground was wonderful. She ran like a quail, and listened like a sleuth-hound at times for the foot-fall of any pursuer.

She was not up to India-rubber soles, perhaps, or her hearing was blunted by her great age, for she went on after each pause, without suspicion. Presently, on the moonlit side of the Written Valley, loomed the wonderful façade of the pink temple; I could see the holes in the rock and the spider-thread of the camel's-hide rope hanging down from the platform. Up the difficult ascent went the prophetess, as nimbly as any spider, in spite of the fact that she carried a bundle tied upon her back, and if she had thought to pull the rope up after her, I should never have crossed the threshold of discovery.

But I was meant to prevent the consummation of her intended crime, and rob the demons she worshipped of a victim. I climbed noiselessly by the road she had travelled, and, sheltered by a group of sandstone pillars, votive offerings for favours received, I looked into the temple. On a bed of ashes before the central altar a fire of wood had been kindled; it roared and blazed as though gum or resin had been smeared upon the fuel. The mummy had been removed from the altar of the goddess with the crescent tiara. At her feet there lay another bundle, covered with a clean, white linen cloth—and the bundle was alive and wriggling feebly under the covering. Then a face of terror came out of the darkness at the other end of the temple, and it belonged to Majendie. He was bareheaded, wearing only a silk shirt and a pair of flannel trousers. At his elbow actively hobbled the hag, Thorah, persuading, entreating, scolding, threatening, persuading him—to what deed I trembled to guess.

"It is nothing, Angleezi. What is the life of a child? A little milk, a few kisses, a little play—then sleep. This one sleeps now; I have given him conserve with *afigoon* (opium). One touch with a sharp blade across the throat, and the babe awakens in Paradise. Also She is greatly propitiated. Be bold. Strike, and win the reward!"

"Strike—and win the reward!" I heard Majendie repeat, in a voice very unlike his own. The withered old witch at his elbow gabbled faster:

"Twice twelve moons ago, and five more, and thou didst prove the truth of my saying. The child Nulad strayed from the tents and tried to climb the Ladder in the Rocks, and fell, and he was dying beyond doubt, and I told thee if thou wouldst carry him up the Ladder and lay him on the altar of the Mother of the Blue Jewels thou shouldst reap a great reward. One of them thou hast on thy finger, blue as Her own eyes, because thou didst bring up the child at my bidding, and lay him here before the breath was out of him, so that She received the oblation of a life. Then thou didst go away and return with the tall yellow-haired Angleezi, whom the girl Aissa loves. Think, did not he spill blood upon the stone, and did not She reward? And again, when thou didst creep here in the silence of the night and open a vein in thy upper arm and pour the hot blood upon Her stone, the Mother of Turquoise smiled on thee. But now she calls for a complete oblation and a sacrifice followed by burnt offerings, for She is thirsty and hungry, and incense has been denied Her nostrils for more than three thousand years. Take this, and throw it into Her fire, and thou shalt see."

The hideous creature had loosed her grasp of Majendie's sleeve to thrust something into his hand, and as he obeyed her fierce, urgent gesture and dropped whatever it was upon the fire, a pungent, fragrant smoke arose and curled in bluish columns towards the carved stone beams of the roof. Clusters of bats, depending from them, broke up and wheeled about wildly, and Thorah clapped her skinny monkey hands and cackled in delight.

"A good omen, Angleezi! All will go well!" Then from under cover of her rags, she plucked a sharp crescent-shaped knife—such a sacrificial knife as the artists of the Egyptian wall-frescoes represented in the hand of the officiating priest—and thrust it upon Majendie. As his nerveless hand closed on the evil-looking thing, the wrinkled face of the hag underwent a hideous convulsion of joy; the cavity of her toothless mouth stretched wide in silent laughter, and suddenly, as she faced me, the bagging folds of flaccid brown skin that filled her orbital cavities were lifted, and— Merciful Powers, what eyes looked forth! Lambent-blue, malignant, devilish!—I have no words in which to describe the horror of that awful gaze. Then the fire leaped higher, and the clouds of incense rolled more heavily, completely enveloping both figures. When I could see again the prophetess had disappeared. I stepped from my place of concealment, meaning to wrest the sacrificial knife from Majendie, who with a deliberate intention expressed in every line of his hitherto nerveless body was now rolling up the sleeve of his silk shirt. And above the level of our heads, upon the broken altar, the drugged child silently squirmed under the linen covering-cloth . . .

"Majendie . . . Arthur, old man! . . . For Heaven's sake don't do it!" I cried, and seized him as he stepped forwards.

He was as strong as twenty men when I grappled with him for the knife. And as our eyes met, I saw that in his stare was no recognition, only the frenzied determination to kill. Twice I tore from him the murderous crescent-blade, twice he wrested it from me, the second time nearly severing the muscles of my left thumb. And, as the warm blood jetted, I distinctly heard a woman's laugh. Not the cackle of the accursed Thorah, but the melodious bell-like laugh of a young woman—a beautiful woman . . .

I glanced upwards. The bas-relief above the central altar, the tablet with the sculptured image of Hathor, was blotted out. In its place was a living splendour, a form of terrible beauty, crowned with the new moon, sheathed

125

in tissues of jewel-hues, her beautiful scarlet lips curved into a cruel smile, her jetty arch of eyebrows vaulting the insupportable blue radiance of the eyes I had seen in my dream. In one hand, golden-tinted, with finger-tips of rose, she held a lotus-bud; in the other a writhing snake. And at her bare and lovely feet writhed the child whose innocent blood those red lips thirsted for, the sacrifice by which alone guerdon of her hidden jewels might be won from the Mother of Turquoise.

I saw the vision first, as I and the man who was my comrade struggled between the sacrificial fire and the sacrificial stone. Majendie must have caught in my dazzled eyes the reflection of that hellish glory, for he glanced over his shoulder, and, loosing his grip of me, swung round to face the altar, and with a gasping cry of rapture and desire, fell upon his knees and stretched out his arms.

"I come not to thee in sleep this time, O my votary," said the slow sweet voice that belonged to those scarlet lips. "With the waking eyes shalt thou and this doubter behold me. Lo! I am waiting the fulfilment of thy vow. Make an end. Strike the blow, and not one but both of ye shall reap the reward that is mine to bestow on those that serve me."

The lotus waved as if beckoning. Majendie rose: in his hand was the knife. He approached the altar. The snake hissed at me as if in warning, and I could not cry out or advance a step from where I stood.

But I could move my right hand, and with a desperate effort I plucked my Colt's revolver out of my hip-pocket, and fired. Straight between those blue, gleaming eyes my bullet sped to its mark. There was a shrill, terrible cry, followed by a heavy, rustling fall, and when the smoke cleared off and the affrighted bats ceased to wheel and dart about my confused eyes I saw that prone upon the altar of Hathor, covering with her dead body the body of the drugged child, the Bedawin sorceress, Thorah, lay face downwards, her crooked finger-tips touching the sandstone floor, upon which, in drifts, lay the light dust of countless ages.

The child Zelim, beyond a bruise or two, was practically unhurt. I carried him down the hide-rope staircase, and then went back for Majendie. I found him delirious and raving, and how I got him down the sheer descent I hardly know.

The Bedawy chief had his youngest-born back again, and in the rejoicings that followed the tribe seemed to overlook the absence of its ancient prophetess. Blind or not, Thorah was a witch of the deepest dye—or else one of the most powerful hypnotists who ever lived. I do not reject either conclusion.

As for Majendie, poor fellow, whom she had so bewildered, he died of fever at Suez, thanking me gratefully almost with his last breath for having saved him from committing an abominable crime. The Turquoise Syndicate were fairly satisfied with the results of their initial venture, but when they wanted me to go out again to the Sinaitic Peninsula and tap the sandstone rocks for fresh deposits of the "blue jewel of Hathor" I declined, and they sent out another man.

I wish him luck with all my heart, but I do not think he is likely to have it. For one thing, the uncanny Thorah is lying dead with a bullet in her brain, over the altar of the pink sandstone temple; and shrivelled to a mummy, I suppose, by now. For another, I paid the Arab to smash all the inscribed tablets within their reach, that I knew advocated the necessity of human blood-sacrifice to the Mother of Turquoise on the part of those who desired to reap riches from her favour. So, even if my successor happens to be a reader of the Egypto-Semitic hieroglyphic character, he will not make out much.

But I am sorry Professor Flanders has been disappointed—really!

The Tooth of Tuloo

The mother of Kolosha, the young *choupan*, said to him when he arose from slumber—

"O thou of the flat nose and shock head, who from thy birth wert consecrated to the priesthood, being buttered with clay and rancid oil, left outside the Kacjimé when it froze hard enough within doors to split a stone, plunged into icy water if thou didst but squall, and whipped with whips of walrus-hide to teach thee endurance! Behold, it is borne in upon me that the time of thy probation is over, and I shall see thee a consecrated high priest, a full-fledged Angakok of the Angakout before I die. To thee will the fairest maidens of our tribe be confided, that thou mayest perfect them in dancing, in beauteous deportment, and the arts of love. Thou wilt boil philtres and cast spells, and make amulets, and smell out witches, and lure the spoil of sea and land to the fish-hook and spear, when the hearts of our hunting men are heavy, and there is no blubber in the land."

Then he who was to become a sorcerer said to his mother—

"By my father's boots (upon which my food was spread when I was a child) thou speakest soothly. For last night, as I wandered over the chill white plains, watching the stars roll through the drifting vapours, and listening to the howling of the wind, the moon looked out from behind a crag that rose up into the black Infinity, and darted a certain ray into my eyeballs. And the hair of my head bristled, and the skin of my flesh crept, for between the crashing of the icebergs and the bellowing of the waves, it seemed that I heard the voice of the Goddess Sidnè—she who lives beneath the sea. And the Ocean Mother cried to me from her throne between the pillars which support the earth—

" 'Kolosha!'

"And I answered, 'Here!'

"And she said, 'Hearken and obey! When next the lamplight flickers on thy waking eyelids, rise up and get thee to the uninhabited Island of the Four Winds, where Tuloo, the dead magician, has slept for nine hundred winters. And there shalt thou receive the revelations and transplant the Wondrous Tooth, and be of the Angakout for evermore. But look to it thou anger not the dead one by any omission of courteous ceremonies, lest thy life pay forfeit for the fault; and thy soul be condemned to wander the chilly wastes of Heaven, with the damned, instead of descending to the snug Paradise that lies deep underground, there to play leapfrog between the pillars, and kiss the comely maidens, and suck blubber with the Blessed for evermore.' "

Thus spake Kolosha, recounting the communication of the Divine One, and his mother, that virtuous woman who had from the first hour of wedlock remained faithful to her husband and his male relations, even to the pitch of carefully cultivating stupidity, ugliness, and uncleanliness, that desires unlawful might be turned away; wept and embraced her son, and fed him with melted grease and seal's entrails, that he might be strong to endure trials; and warmed his feet in her bosom ere he went forth from the hut.

And he took his paddle and went to the beach and launched a little boat of sealskins, and invoked Jug Jak, the

Father of All Whales, for safety on the voyage; and sped over the black water to the Island of the Four Winds. And he drew up the *kaiak* on the ice-floe and hid the paddle; and went over the sharp rocks to the cave where for nine hundred winters Tuloo the Old had slept; and legions of spirits battled in the sky overhead so that the glancing of their spears dazzled the eyeballs of Kolosha, and the clouds were dyed with their crimson blood.

And coming to the entrance of the cave, he struck fire from flint and lighted a wisp of moss, and stuck it in a shellful of oil and entered. And behold! the Ancient sat there, dry and mummified, wearing a mask, and clad in his sorcerer's robes. The wings of a screech-owl were outspread above his hood of sable marten fur, and his outer garment of white dressed deer-skin was fringed with ivory marmosets, foxes and penguins; and his gloves were of otter-fur, while his boots were bordered with bells, little and big, and he wore a breastplate of chains and rings, eagles' claws and fishes' scales, and a girdle of walrus teeth. And he held the Holy Drum betwixt the stiff knees of him; and upon it the Cross of the Four Winds and the Eye of Sidnè the All-seeing were delineated, and magical clay figures of men and women and animals were hidden inside. And Kolosha, broadening his heart with a deep breath (for the Dead was terrible to look upon) cried—

"Hail! Hear! Respond!" and struck upon the magic Drum so that the puppets inside rattled and squeaked.

And at the noise the owl's feathers fluttered, and the mask shook, and the corpse started—but Kolosha was not afraid.

And he struck upon the Drum a second time. And the wind roared, and the rocks rumbled, and the serried lights in the northern sky leapt up and went out. But the little oil lamp glimmered bravely and Kolosha did not tremble.

And he struck upon the Drum a third time, and the roof of the cavern split, and the sky became a sheet of fire, and the sea heaved and was troubled, and rose up like a wall all round the island, and crested over a black wave-curl edged with foam, as if about to overwhelm it. But Kolosha knew no fear.

And he cried, "With Permission!" and put forth his hand and removed the headdress and undid the mask of the corpse and laid it aside, and looked in the face of the black grinning mummy and met with his living eyes the rayless stare of death.

And he saluted Tuloo with a formal salutation, rubbing noses with him, and patting him upon the stomach; and he spat in his palms and anointed his countenance with saliva—a compliment which is only paid to the most honourable persons—and made an offering of three pipefuls of tobacco, and the raw liver of a bear, which sickens men that eat of it and slays dogs outright. And at sight of these delicacies Tuloo smiled with lips that were like yellow parchment, and nodded so that the little sticks fixed in the top of his skull rattled together.

Then the heart of Kolosha was lifted up, for he perceived that his offerings were graciously accepted, and he made obeisance thrice and lowlily, and cried, "Inculcate! I await!" and squatted at the feet of the mummy. And he sought wisdom of Tuloo, asking, "Where liveth Perfection?"

And Tuloo spake not, but the answer was written upon his forehead in luminous letters that shone and shifted and vanished as Kolosha looked upon them.

"Nowhere upon Earth. For never yet was man nor woman born that sinned not. The best of the Human Kind are bad in spots. Remember this and trust not fully."

And Kolosha spake again, asking, "Where exists Absolute Evil?"

And the answer lightened out again upon the forehead-bone of Tuloo—

"Nowhere upon Earth. For never yet lived man nor woman that was entirely wicked. The worst of the Human Kind are good in patches. Remember this and doubt not wholly."

And Kolosha said, "Frost and fire, weeping and laughter, pleasure and pain, poison and nourishment, health and disease. What is this?"

And Tuloo answered, "This is Love; for it freezes and warms, rejoices and grieves, it kills and cherishes, raises up and casts down. Hast thou no harder question, Kolosha?"

And Kolosha said, "An empty pot and a full pot, a lamp that smokes and one that burns clear, a rotten blanket and one that is sound, a leaky canoe and a taut boat. What signifies this?"

And the dead man returned, "This is Life. To one man sweet, to another bitter, according to the measure he receives. Tax me with something tougher, Kolosha!"

And Kolosha lifted his head and cried, "The End and the Beginning, the day-set and the dawn, the Defeat and the Victory. The Certainty that was Doubt and the Doubt which is Certainty. The Sleep which is Waking and the Waking that is Sleep. O, Tuloo! tell me what is this?"

And Tuloo answered, "This is Death. And weary me with no more questions, for I would slumber with the dead again. Take the tooth thou camest for, and with it wisdom, and begone."

And he opened his mouth and yawned, and Kolosha saw the tooth sticking whole and sound in the rotting jaw, and put forth an eager hand to take it.

But in his haste and greed he forgot to say "With Permission", and the dead sorcerer was angered at his lack of manners and snapped his jaws together, catching the finger of Kolosha, so that it was bitten to the bone. And Kolosha bore the pain without flinching, for he had been schooled to endure; and politely begged the corpse's leave to depart.

But Tuloo said in the writing that was written upon his forehead-bone, "For nine hundred winters have I sat me here, and many sons of men have come to me to receive enlightenment and to borrow a tooth, but none strove to grab the treasure from my mouth without asking permission. Art a rude fellow, and I will not set thee free! The long nights and the long days shall come and go, and moons shall wax and moons shall wane, and suns shall wake from wintry sleep and glad the waiting world with warm and greenness. But here thou shalt tarry, Kolosha, and live till thou diest, and shrivel when thou art dead to a mummy like me!"

And hearing this Kolosha whipped out a sharp little knife of bone and would have cut off his finger. But the heart of Tuloo softened and he bade him hold, saying—

"One chance thou shalt have for thy finger. In life, O Kolosha, are many good things; but the best thing of all to the Inoit is laughter. And while I lived I laughed much. At the fat that spluttered in the cooking pot, when the lamp-flame licked it; at the end of my nose when it froze and fell off; at the narwhal that was driven ashore by the gale, when we ate our way into his belly and came out all crimson on the other side; at the famine that came and starved us to skin and bone, so that a man rattled in his garments like a dried berry in a bladder. Little else asked I but laughter, and now I am dead and laugh no more. Tell me three merry tales, and if thou canst make me laugh, even with one of them, I will free thy finger, I swear it by Sidnè, the mother of the Father of Whales, and Tornasouk of the Holy Drum! But if I cackle not, nor chuckle, nor so much as grin, by the third essay—then here thou shalt stay with me, Kolosha, while life endures, or win home without thy finger, and the Wisdom thou didst seek!"

And Kolosha pondered a space and said, "Hear the story of the Frugal Wife!

"A man returned from the chase without spoil of fish or fowl. And when he saw his wife trudging through the mud in her big boots—'*Sook-sook*'—to meet him, between hunger and disappointment his gall overflowed, and he harpooned her violently, crying, 'By Sidnè! it shall not be said that I have hit nothing to-day!' But the sharp weapon, failing to pierce the thickness of the woman's clothing, rebounded from her outer garment, which was made of a bear's skin, leaving but a rent, and she, turning round without a word, went upon her way; and the man, being ashamed of his violence, did no more. But on the morrow he went forth again and caught much fish; and when he paddled home his wife came out to meet him, as it is the duty of a wife to do. But while yet afar she paused, and cried, 'Fortune or none?' And the man, meaning to be merry with her, answered, 'Meaner sport than yesterday!' Upon which she cried again, saying, 'O thou honourable and greasy one! Suffer that I return home and put on the garment in which thou didst harpoon me yesterday, so that this, which is new and without a rent, may not be spoiled!' Thus she spake in her frugality and the tale has been told for an example since."

So he ended, and Tuloo did not laugh, but only bit the finger more sharply and said: "Vanity rather than frugality, and a poor tale, moreover; one without the shake of a rib in it. Tell thou a better if thou wouldst wend free."

And Kolosha said (having reflected awhile): "Hear the story of the Greedy Man!

"An envious and greedy man passed by the hut of a generous and unselfish one, and such a savoury odour smelled he that he crawled down the passage and thrust his head between the bear-skins. And the sight he saw made his mouth water. For the host was sitting to banquet with his family and friends, and before them were spread pieces of whale's flesh rolled in blubber, putrid dried fish, and mince of raw seal's liver, sprinkled with live maggots—"

Here Kolosha broke off the tale, for Tuloo gibbered with wrath and nipped the finger bitterly and said, "Enough. Is it not sufficiently bad to know that I am dead and shall never eat earthly food again, without being taunted with talk of all these savoury viands? Skip the banquet and go on."

Said Kolosha, with the tears standing in his eyes, from the pain of his finger—

"Only two more dishes were there, O Majestical Mummied One!—reindeer's marrow, and bilberries mashed with grease and snow. And to wash these down, great goblets of rancid oil of a very superior brand. *Ou-ie!*"

This because Tuloo had bitten the finger again.

"And so the host called to the greedy man to enter and sit at his right hand. And the greedy one did so gladly, but observing the host thrust his hand into the best dish and draw out the most delicate morsel, '*That he means to eat himself,*' he thought, and in his spite, secretly rubbed the tit-bit with a piece of human fat he carried about him, taken from a grave he had violated in order to procure this powerful charm. But to his surprise and shame, the envied mouthful was thrust between his own lips, and in confusion he swallowed it, not daring to refuse. But no sooner had it passed his gullet than a raging hunger seized him, and he fell upon the dishes and cleared them one after the other and drank up the oil, goblets and all; and would have eaten the guests, by virtue of the evil spell, had they not fled in terror. Upon which he himself ran home, and, meeting his young children by the way, devoured them; and then fell upon his wife and made short work of her; and then ate his dogs and his skins, his great hide boots and his very sledges. Finally, when nothing else was left to devour, he gobbled up his mother-in-law and died of an indigestion. He, he, he!"

It was Kolosha who chuckled and not the corpse. In truth a ripple such as one sees upon the surface of dark waters over which a wandering breeze passes, stirred the face of the Ancient, but he made no other sign, save in squeezing more closely the finger of Kolosha between his jagged jaws, so that the youth's grin was speedily changed to a grimace of anguish.

And Tuloo said, "Of thy chances two are gone, O miserable one! If I laugh not the next time thou art a doomed man!"

Upon which Kolosha, hiding his dread with a show of indifference, cast about in his memory for a side-splitting story, but behold! the mirth had gone out of all those he remembered, so that they seemed as mouldy and as stale as the six months' dead papoose that is carried at the back of the mourning mother in its cradle of birch-bark and moss.

And he gulped and faltered and said, "Hear the tale and read the riddle of the Polite Penguin, that was told to the child Chulik by the fool Falesha!

"A penguin waddling home to the seashore, in haste to lay an egg, met with a blue fox on his way back from the fishing; and immediately, despite the pressing nature of her business, turned back with the animal. But whereas she had set out shorewards on two legs, she returned inland on four! O, Tuloo! canst thou read the riddle?"

And Tuloo pondered a while, and at last he said, "What have I to do with a fool's riddle? Guess the answer for thyself, and I will tell thee whether thou art right or wrong.

How should the bird that went forth on two legs return upon four?"

And Kolosha spake and answered, "Because, O Venerable Dried Up One! the penguin travelled inside the fox!"

And Tuloo was taken unawares and his jaws fell apart, releasing the finger of Kolosha from durance sore; and he laughed a whistling laugh, and shook until his ribs rattled in his skin. And Kolosha snatched from the wide open mouth of the mummy the august tooth and clapped it into his own, and hid it under his tongue, and became upon the instant an Angakok by virtue of its power.

And Tuloo said, "Get thee hence with thy dear-bought wisdom, Kolosha! Yet ere thou goest tell me the first truth the tooth hath taught thee."

And Kolosha made answer, "It is that the wisdom of the wisest may be baffled by the folly of a fool. For thou who knowest the secrets of the stars and the language of the winds, and canst pierce into the Past and foretell the Future, couldst not read the riddle of Falesha."

And he quitted the cave and went back to the shore, and found the sea quiet, and his boat as he had left it. And he departed from the Island of the Four Winds and returned to the country of the Inoit.

The Great Beast of Kafue

It happened at our homestead on the border of Southeastern Rhodesia, seventy miles from Tuli Concession, some three years after the War.

A September storm raged, the green, broad-leaved tobacco-plants tossed like the waves of the ocean I had crossed and re-crossed, journeying to and coming back from my dead mother's wet, sad country of Ireland to this land of my father and his father's father.

The acacias and kameel thorns and the huge cactus-like euphorbia that fringed the water-courses and the irrigation channels had wrung their hands all day without ceasing, like Makalaka women at a native funeral. Night closed in: the wooden shutters were barred, the small-paned windows fastened, yet they shook and rattled as though human beings without were trying to force a way in. Whitewash fell in scales from the big tie-beams and cross-rafters of the farm kitchen, and lay in little powdery drifts of whiteness on the solid table of brown locust-tree wood, and my father's Dutch Bible that lay open there. Upon my father's great black head that was bent over the Book, were many streaks and patches of white that might not be shaken or brushed away.

It had fallen at the beginning of the War, that snow of sorrow streaking the heavy curling locks of coarse black hair. My pretty young mother—an Irishwoman of the North, had been killed in the Women's Laager at Gueldersdorp during the Siege. My father served as Staats gunner during the investment—and now you know the dreadful doubt that heaped upon those mighty shoulders a bending load, and sprinkled the black hair with white.

You are to see me in my blue drill roundabout and little homespun breeches sitting on a cricket in the shadow of the table-ledge, over against the grim *sterk* figure in the big, thong-seated armchair.

There would be no going to bed that night. The dam was over-full already, and the next spate from the hill sluits might crack the great wall of mud-cemented saw-squared boulders, or overflow it, and lick away the work of years. The farm-house roof had been rebuilt since the shell from the English naval gun had wrecked it, but the work of men to-day is not like that of the men of old. My father shook his head, contemplating the new masonry, and the whitewash fell as though in confirmation of his expressed doubts.

I had begged to stay up rather than lie alone in the big bed in my father's room. Nodding with sleepiness I should have denied, I carved with my two-bladed American knife at a little canoe I meant to swim in the shallower river-pools. And as I shaped the prow I dreamed of something I had heard on the previous night.

A traveller of the better middle-class, overseer of a coal-mine working "up Bulawayo" way, who had stayed with us the previous night and gone on to Tuli that morning, had told the story. What he had failed to tell I had haltingly spelled out of the three-weeks-old English newspaper he had left behind.

So I wrought, and remembered, and my little canoe swelled and grew in my hands. I was carrying it on my back through a forest of tall reeds and high grasses, forcing a painful way between the tough wrist-thick stems, with the salt sweat running down into my eyes . . . Then I was in the canoe, wielding the single paddle, working my frail crank craft through sluggish pools of black water, overgrown with broad spiny leaves of water-plants cradling flowers of marvellous hue. In the canoe bows leaned my grandfather's elephant-gun, the inlaid, browned-steel-barrelled weapon with the diamond-patterned stock and breech, that had always seemed to my childish eyes the most utterly desirable, absolutely magnificent possession a grown-up man might call his own.

A *paauw* made a great commotion getting up amongst the reeds; but does a hunter go after *paauw* with his grandfather's elephant-gun? Duck were feeding in the open spaces of sluggish black water. I heard what seemed to be the plop! of a jumping fish, on the other side of a twenty-foot high barrier of reeds and grasses. I looked up then, and saw, glaring down upon me from inconceivable heights of sheer horror, the Thing of which I had heard and read.

At this juncture I dropped the little canoe and clutched my father round the leg.

"What is it, *mijn jongen?*"

He, too, seemed to rouse out of a waking dream. You are to see the wide, burnt-out-looking grey eyes that were staring sorrowfully out of their shadowy caves under the shaggy eyebrows, lighten out of their deep abstraction and drop to the level of my childish face.

"You were thinking of the great beast of Kafue Valley, and you want to ask me if I will lend you my father's elephant-rifle when you are big enough to carry it that you may go and hunt for the beast and kill it; is that so?"

My father grasped his great black beard in one huge knotted brown hand, and made a rope of it, as was his way. He looked from my chubby face to the old-fashioned black-powder 8-bore that hung upon the wall against a leopard kaross, and back again, and something like a smile curved the grim mouth under the shaggy black and white moustache.

"The gun you shall have, boy, when you are of age to use it, or a 450-Mannlicher or a 600-Mauser, the best that may be bought north of the Transvaal, to shoot explosive or conical bullets from cordite cartridges. But not unless you give me your promise never to kill that beast, shall money of mine go to the buying of such a gun for you. Come now, let me have your word!"

Even to my childish vanity the notion of my solemnly entering into a compact binding my hand against the slaying of the semi-fabulous beast-marvel of the Upper Rhodesian swamps, smacked of the fantastic if not of the absurd. But my father's eyes had no twinkle in them, and I faltered out the promise they commanded.

"*Nooit—nooit* will I kill that beast! It should kill me, rather!"

"Your mother's son will not be *valsch* to a vow. For so would you, son of my body, make of me, your father, a traitor to an oath that I have sworn!"

The great voice boomed in the rafters of the farm kitchen, vying with the baffled roaring of the wind that was trying to get in, as I had told myself, and lie down, folding wide quivering wings and panting still, upon the sheepskin that was spread before the hearth.

"But—but why did you swear?"

I faltered out the question, staring at the great bearded figure in homespun jacket and tan-cord breeches and *veldschoens*, and thought again that it had the hairy skin of Esau and the haunted face of Saul.

Said my father, grimly—

"Had I questioned my father so at twice your age, he would have skinned my back and I should have deserved it. But I cannot beat your mother's son, though the Lord punish me for my weakness . . . And you have the spirit of the *jager* in you, even as I. What I saw you may one day see. What I might have killed, that shall you spare, because of me and my oath. Why did I take it upon me, do you ask? Even though I told you, how should a child understand? What is it you are saying? Did I really, really see the beast? Ay, by the Lord!" said my father thoughtfully, "I saw him. And never can a man who has seen, forget that sight. What are you saying?"

The words tumbled over one another as I stammered in my hurry—

"But—but the English traveller said only one white man besides the Mashona hunter has seen the beast, and the newspaper says so too."

"*Natuurlijk.* And the white man is me," thundered the deep voice.

I hesitated.

"But since the planting of the tobacco you have not left the *plaats.* And the newspaper is of only three weeks back."

"*Dat spreekt,* but the story is older than that, *mijn jongen.* It is the third time it has been dished up in the *Bulawayo Courant* sauced up with lies to change the taste as belly-lovers have their meat. But I am the man who saw the beast of Kafue, and the story that is told is my story, nevertheless!"

I felt my cheeks beginning to burn. Wonderful as were the things I knew to be true of the man, my father, this promised to be the most wonderful of all.

"It was when I was hunting in the Zambezi Country," said my father, "three months after the *Commandaants* of the Forces of the United Republics met at Klerksdorp to arrange conditions of peace—"

"With the English Generals," I put in.

142

"With the English, as I have said. You had been sent to your—to *her* people in Ireland. I had not then thought of rebuilding the farm. For more than a house of stones had been thrown down for me, and more than so many thousand acres of land laid waste . . .

"Where did I go? *Ik wiet niet.* I wandered *op en neer* like the evil spirit in the Scriptures," the great corded hand shut the Book and reached over and snuffed the tallow-dip that hung over at the top, smoking and smelling, and pitched the black wick-end angrily on the red hearth embers. "I sought rest and found none, either for the sole of my foot or the soul in my body. There is bitterness in my mouth as though I have eaten the spotted lily-root of the swamps. I cannot taste the food I swallow, and when I lie down at night something lies down with me, and when I rise up, it rises too and goes by my side all day."

I clung to the leg of the table, not daring to clutch my father's. For his eyes did not seem to see me any more, and a blob of foam quivered on his beard that hung over his great breast in a shadowy cascade dappled with patches of white. He went on, I scarcely daring to breathe—

"For, after all, do I know it is not I who killed her? That accursed day, was I not on duty as ever since the beginning of the investment, and is it not a splinter from a Maxim Nordenfeld fired from an eastern gun-position, that—" Great drops stood on my father's forehead. His huge frame shook. The clenched hand resting on the solid table of locust-beam, shook that also, shaking me, clinging to the table-leg with my heart thumping violently, and a cold, crawling sensation among the roots of my curls.

"At first, I seem to remember there was a man hunting with me. He had many Kaffir servants and four Mashona hunters and wagons drawn by salted tailless spans, fine guns and costly tents, plenty of stores and medicine in little sugar-pills, in bottles with silver tops. But he sickened in spite of all his quinine, and the salted oxen died, just like beasts with tails; and besides, he was afraid of the Makwakwa and the Mashengwa with their slender poisoned spears of reeds. He turned back at last. I pushed on."

There was a pause. The strange, iron-grey, burnt-out eyes looked through me and beyond me, then the deep, trembling voice repeated, once more changing the past into the present tense—

"I push on west. My life is of value to none. The boy— is he not with her people? Shall I live to have him back under my roof and see in his face one day the knowledge that I have killed his mother? Nay, nay, I will push on!"

There was so long a silence after this that I ventured to move. Then my father looked at me, and spoke to me, not as though I were a child, but as if I had been another man.

"I pushed on, crossing the rivers on a blown-up goatskin and some calabashes, keeping my father's elephant-gun and my cartridges dry by holding them above my head. Food! For food there were thorny orange cucumbers with green pulp, and the native women at the kraals gave me cakes of maize and milk. I hunted and killed rhino and elephant and hippo and lion until the head-men of the Mashengwa said the beast was a god of theirs and the slaying of it would bring a pestilence upon their tribe, and so I killed no more. And one day I shot a cow hippo with her calf, and she stood to suckle the ugly little thing while her life was bleeding out of her, and after that I ceased to kill. I needed little, and there were yet the green-fleshed cucumbers, and ground-nuts, and things like those."

He made a rope of his great beard, twisting it with a rasping sound.

"Thus I reached the Upper Kafue Valley where the great grass swamps are. No railway then, running like an iron snake up from Bulawayo to bring the ore down from the silver-mines that are there.

"Six days' *trek* from the mines—I went on foot always, you will understand!—six days' journey from the mines, above where L'uengwe River is wedded to Kafue, as the Badanga say—is a big water.

"It is a lake, or rather, two lakes, not round, but shaped like the bowls of two wooden spoons. A shore of black, stone-like baked mud round them, and a bridge of the same stone is between them, so that they make the figure that is for eight."

The big, hairy forefinger of my father's right hand traced the numeral in the powdered whitewash that lay in drifts upon the table.

"That is the shape of the lakes, and the Badanga say that they have no bottom, and that fish taken from their waters remain raw and alive, even on the red-hot embers of their cooking stove. They are a lazy, dirty people who live on snakes and frogs and grubs—tortoise and fish. And they gave me to eat and told me, partly in words of my own *moder* Taal they had picked up somehow, partly in sign language, about the Great Beast that lives in the double lake that is haunted by the spirits of their dead."

I waited, my heart pumping at the bottom of my throat, my blood running horribly, delightfully chill, to hear the rest.

"The hunting spirit revives in a man, even at death's door, to hear of an animal the like of which no living hunter has ever brought down. The Badanga tell me of this one, tales, tales, tales! They draw it for me with a pointed stick on a broad green leaf, or in the ashes of their cooking fires. And I have seen many a great beast, but, *voor den donder*! never a beast such as that!"

I held on to my stool with both hands.

"I ask the Badanga to guide me to the lair of the beast for all the money I have upon me. They care not for gold, but for the old silver hunting-watch I carry they will risk offending the spirits of their dead. The old man who has drawn the creature for me, he will take me. And it is January, the time of year in which he has been before known to rise and bellow—*Maar!*—bellow like twenty buffalo bulls in spring-time, for his mate to rise from those bottomless deeps below and drink the air and sun."

So there are two great beasts! Neither the traveller nor the newspaper nor my father, until this moment, had hinted at that!

"The she-beast is much the smaller and has no horns. This my old man makes clear to me, drawing her with the point of his fish-spear on smooth mud. She is very sick the last time my old man has seen her. Her great moon-eyes are dim, and the stinking spume dribbles from her jaws. She can only float in the trough of the wave that her mate makes with his wallowings, her long scaly neck lying like a dead python on the oily black water. My old man thinks she was then near death. I ask him how long ago that is? Twenty times have the blue lake-lilies blossomed, the lilies with the sweet seeds that the Badanga make bread of— since. And the great bull has twice been heard bellowing, but never has he been seen of man since then."

My father folded his great arms upon the black-and-white cascade of beard that swept down over his shirt of homespun and went on—

"Twenty years. Perhaps, think I, my old man has lied to me! But we are at the end of the last day's journey. The sun has set and night has come. My old man makes me signs we are near the lakes and I climb a high mahogo, holding by the limbs of the wild fig that is hugging the tree to death."

My father spat into the heart of the glowing wood ashes, and said—

"I see the twin lakes lying in the midst of the high grass-swamps, barely a mile away. The black, shining waters cradle the new moon of January in their bosom, and the blue star that hangs beneath her horn, and there is no ripple on the surface, or sign of a beast, big or little. And I despise myself, I, the son of honest Booren, who have been duped by the lies of a black man-ape. I am coming down the tree, when through the night comes a long, hollow, booming, bellowing roar that is not the cry of any beast I know. Thrice it comes, and my old man of the Badanga, squatting among the roots of the mahogo, nods his wrinkled bald skull, and says, squinting up at me, 'Now you have heard, Baas, will you go back or go on?'

"I answer, '*Al recht uit!*'

"For something of the hunting spirit has wakened in me. And I see to the cleaning of the elephant-gun and load it carefully before I sleep that night."

I would have liked to ask a question but the words stuck in my throat.

"By dawn of day we have reached the lakes," went on my father. "The high grass and the tall reeds march out into the black water as far as they may, then the black stone beach shelves off into depths unknown.

"He who has written up the story for the Bulawayo newspaper says that the lake was once a volcano and that the crumbly black stone is lava. It may be so. But volcanoes are holes in the tops of mountains, while the lakes lie in a valley-bottom, and he who wrote cannot have been there, or he would know there are two, and not one.

"All the next night we, camping on the belt of stony shore that divides lake from lake, heard nothing. We ate the parched grain and baked grubs that my old man carried in a little bag. We lighted no fire because of the spirits of the dead Badanga that would come crowding about it to warm themselves, and poison us with their breath. My old man said so, and I humoured him. My dead needed no fire to bring her to me. She was there always . . .

"All the day and the night through we heard and saw nothing. But at windstill dawn of the next day I saw a great curving ripple cross the upper lake that may be a mile and a half wide; and the reeds upon the nearer shore were wetted to the knees as by the wave that is left in the wake of a steamer, and oily patches of scum, each as big as a barn floor, befouled the calm water, and there was a cold, strange smell upon the breeze, but nothing more.

"Until at sunset of the next day, when I stood upon the mid-most belt of shore between lake and lake, with my back to the blood-red wonder of the west and my eyes sheltered by my hand as I looked out to where I had seen the waters divided as a man furrows earth with the ploughshare, and felt a shadow fall over me from behind, and turned . . . and saw . . . *Alamachtig!*"

I could not breathe. At last, at last, it was coming!

"I am no coward," said my father, in his deep resounding bass, "but that was a sight of terror. My old man of the Badanga had bolted like a rock-rabbit. I could hear the dry reeds crashing as he broke through. And the horned head of the beast, that was as big as a wagon-trunk shaking about on the top of a python-neck that topped the tallest of the teak-trees or mahogos that grow in the grass-swamps, seemed as if it were looking for the little human creature that was trying to run away.

"*Voor den donder!* how the water rises up in columns of smoke-spray as the great beast lashes it with his crocodile tail! His head is crocodile also, with horns of rhino, his body has the bulk of six hippo bulls together. He is covered with armour of scales, yellow-white as the scales of leprosy, he has paddles like a tortoise. God of my fathers, what a beast to see! I forget the gun I hold against my hip—I can only stand and look, while the cold, thick puffs of stinking musk are brought to my nostrils and my ear-drums are well-nigh split with the bellowing of the beast. Ay! and the wave of his wallowings that wets one to the neck is foul with clammy ooze and oily scum.

"Why did the thing not see me? I did not try to hide from those scaly-lidded great eyes, yellow with half-moon shaped pupils, I stood like an idol of stone. Perhaps that saved me, or I was too little a thing to vent a wrath so great upon. He who in the beginning made herds of beasts like that to move upon the face of the waters, and let this one live to show the pigmy world of to-day what creatures were of old, knows. I do not. I was dazed with the noise of its roarings and the thundering blows of its huge tail upon the water; I was drenched with the spume of its snortings and sickened with the stench it gave forth. But I never took my eyes from it, as it spent its fury, and little by little I came to understand.

"*Het is jammer* to see anything suffer as that beast was suffering. Another man in my place would have thought as much, and when it lay still at last on the frothing black water, a bullet from the elephant-rifle would have lodged in the little stupid brain behind the great moon-eye, and there would have been an end . . .

"But I did not shoot!"

It seemed an age before my father spoke again, though the cuckoo-clock had only ticked eight times.

"No! I would not shoot and spare the beast, dinosaurus or brontosaurus, or whatever the wiseacres who have not seen him may name him, the anguish that none had spared me. '*Let him go on!*' said I. '*Let him go on seeking her in the abysses that no lead-line may ever fathom, without consolation, without hope! Let him rise to the sun and the breeze of spring through miles of the cold black water, and find her not, year after year until the ending of the world. Let him call her through the mateless nights until Day and Night rush together at the sound of the Trumpet of the Judgment, and Time shall be no more!'"*

Crash!

The great hand came down upon the solid locust-wood table, breaking the spell that had bound my tongue.

"I—do not understand," I heard my own child-voice saying. "Why was the Great Beast so sorry? What was he looking for?"

"His mate who died. Ay, at the lower end of the second lake, where the water shallows, her bones were sticking up like the bleached timbers of a wrecked ship. And He and She being the last of their kind upon the earth, therefore he knows desolation . . . and shall know it till death brings forgetfulness and rest. Boy, the wind is fallen, the rain has spent itself, it is time that you go to bed."

The Friend

1919

The five years' night-and-daymare of the Great War was over. Victory crowned the flags of the Allies. All the bells of grey old London town were ringing crazily for joy. Venetian masts strung with the colours of the Entente, the Dominions, and America, and wreathed with evergreens and flowers, marked out the route of the Pageant of Triumph. The atmosphere throbbed with salutes of great guns, and vibrated with cheers and military music. Between the houses of the familiar streets all adorned with bunting and transparencies and garlands and streamers, between the packed and crowded stands, and the surging crowd pent in behind lines of bronzed troops and bluejackets, and the broad backs of Metropolitan policemen, came the war-worn, war-toughened, war-scarred men of the Service to give thanks to God for victory, under the grey reverberating dome that covers the glorious dust of Nelson and Wellington.

It seemed to Kittums that she hated the rejoicings. Let happy girls go whose sweethearts had come back to them out of the German fire of annihilation, and happier women who had got back their sons and brothers and husbands. She did not grudge those others their joy—she only asked not to have to see it. So while the sweet wild madness of the bells set the air vibrating, and the guns boomed forth salutes, and the sanded streets were full of people flocking to take up their places for the triumph, she lay with shut eyes on the sofa at home. When she opened her eyes, a tall, brown-bearded man in khaki was sitting by her pillow. His face was indistinct to Kittums's view, but his mere presence filled her with content.

"Who are you?" she whispered by and by. He took her hand and raised her up and said to her quietly:

"Who I am does not matter. It is enough that I am your Friend. Come out with me into the streets and learn why you should rejoice as well as others." And when she held back, his irresistible strength constrained her. She found herself compelled to obey.

O! the glorious sunshine pouring streams of gold on the long files of passing bayonets. The proud trampling of cavalry squadrons and the trot and clink and roll of the oncoming batteries and the roar of welcome from a million throats . . .

Kittums shut her eyes and thrust her fingers in her ears to keep out sight and sound of what was coming. They had taken her as a child of seven to see the return of the British Forces at the end of the South African War. Oh! the empty saddles with the spurred boots reversed, and the heartbreaking gaps in the passing squadrons. Oh! the pitifulness of the empty spaces in the infantry columns that went swinging by. Famous batteries of field artillery were represented by a gun or two. The weather-stained caps of the dead men were piled upon the limbers, the sight had turned even the seven-years baby that Kittums had been then, deadly sick and clammily cold.

A woman now, in a widow's trailing veil, she grew furious with misery. She would have liked to dash her clenched hand in the beaming open-mouthed faces that she saw about her whenever she used her eyes. She knelt down in the dust and clasped her hands, praying the Friend to take her home. But he raised her up, sternly though gently. By some strange, irresistible power he compelled her to obey.

"Do you not see, my child," he said to her as the thinned batteries and the decimated battalions went by, amidst the deafening plaudits, "that the happiest faces about you belong to those who are dressed in black?"

And it was as he had said. The old men with bowed shoulders and crêpe armlets, the grey-haired motherly women in dusty mourning, the widows in their floating black veils were the most radiant of all. One, thin and young, and smiling, held up a little child that kicked in ecstasy, gurgling "daddy", pointing with its dimpled hand to an empty space where no man walked. Grief must have driven the woman mad, and upon the brain of her child were stamped her delusions. How terrible, how pitiful it all was. Far worse than Kittums had feared!

Now aeroplanes and seaplanes flew singing overhead, the flying men of both Services marched under the triumphal arches, and in their ranks were ugly holes where men, like teeth, had been plucked out. Her brother Arthur was not there, though Kittums strained her eyes for him. Then she remembered:

"He is dead like Franky! How shall I bear it when the Guards pass, and my dear soldier is not with them. O, how I hope they have already gone by!" But a shout went up that the Guards were coming, and she tried to shut her eyes, but could not . . . The White Tufts and the Cut Red Feathers passed to the blare of martial music, and the thunder of human throats; and it was as though Death had been reaping, here and there at random great patches in a field of tall brown corn.

"Be patient.—Wait only a little longer," said the unknown friend, as with the flutter of one royal tartan and the skirl of "Hieland Laddie" the Bearskins Plain, third regiment of the glorious brigade, came marching down the stately thoroughfare under the wreaths and fluttering flags and garlands, and a fresh outburst of popular acclamation made the walls shake and quiver about them and the garlands dance in the bright air. The Friend leaned over and touched her brow, and a wonderful thrill went through her. Her soldier, her Franky—could he be coming? Was it true, that for Kittums as for the other people in war-mourning, the places of their beloved, lost ones, were not to be empty that day?

It was true. True. O, merciful God! For here came the familiar, worshipped face, the well-known figure, marching with his company of the glorious first battalion. More handsome than she had ever dreamed, more splendid, and more strong . . . The brown eyes were all for her, with what a radiant smile in them. "*My love,*" the gentle mouth seemed ready to say, "how well we understand each other now!"

"Hurrah!—hurrah!" Kittums waved her handkerchief and cheered, sobbing and laughing wildly. As the beloved passed beyond sight she looked up, smiling, into the eyes of the Friend.

Washed by the joyful tears they had shed, her eyes discerned his Face more clearly. It was luminous as a white flame, and glorious beyond words. And his robe was whiter than linen steeped in the Lys, and mighty wings arched from his shoulders . . . "Did you not know Death was your Friend?" said a voice whose resonant sweetness seemed to drown out all other voices. And Kittums awakened, crying for joy.

Dark Dawn

Upchyme is a lonely little village of a dozen cottages, a Methodist meeting-house, and a post-office, perched in a niche amongst the cliffs, a mile southward of the little sea-coast market town of Chyme, in West Barset. The beaten cart-track that leads to it forks off in a gradual ascent to Ragbert's Castle—an entrenchment of Roman type, crowning a grassy shoulder of the hills eight hundred feet above sea-level. Tourists now seldom visit the castle; the climb is stiff for bicycles, the path narrows for traps and motors; but local patronage is not withheld, the very first walk taken by a maid with her sweetheart, or a newly-married wife with her husband, being in this direction. When on an autumn day in 1899 Temperance Upwey and Corporal Ramsall Cane, over the courting-stage and walking hand-in-hand, came in sight of the outer line of earthworks that crowned the steep, the girl gave a little start and cry, and Ramsall said, squeezing the soft, clinging hand:

"Why, Tempy, you make as if you'd never seen th' place before."

"Nor do I feel as though I had," answered the girl with a soft, rich laugh, a fluty thrush-note of joy and exultation thrilling in it. " 'Tis as though everything were new made over like since yesterday."

"For you and for me," said Ramsall with the aptness of a lover in the early stages of acceptance. He dropped her

155

hand. "I'll race you to th' first ditch," he said exultantly, "as I used when we were boy and maid. Take twenty yards' start—let our mark be that clump of thyme." He snapped his fingers. "Once, twice, and away with you!" he cried; and Temperance, turning a bright face upon him for an instant, filled her lungs with a deep inspiration and darted up the grassy steep. The corporal held back, measuring her flight until the twenty yards were covered; then he ran forward swiftly in pursuit. Dressed as he was in easily-fitting khaki, for the West Barset Regiment had been notified for active service, and would sail for South Africa within the month, the fine muscles of his body and limbs had free play, and his feet, shod with strong but light brown leather, padded the sunburnt turf as easily, if not as clingingly, as though they had been bare. For the pleasure of the laughter and sweet argument that should ensue, he held back from gaining upon Temperance's flying feet, and was still half-a-dozen yards behind her when she passed the clump of thyme. He heard her laugh, triumphant and gay, as she threw up her hand in sign of his defeat; he saw her spring through the narrow entrance in the earthwork and disappear. Then he launched forward at speed, passed the thyme-clump in a twinkling, and leaped between the grassy banks in pursuit of Temperance. She was not in sight.

"Why, wher've the maid gone?" the corporal cried, lapsing into the local dialect in his momentary surprise. He turned the angle of the second line of earthworks, and then he saw her, standing, slim and straight and black against the strong rays of the westering sun. One arm hung by her side, the hand of the other shaded her eyes, the line of her throat was tense with the angle at which she tilted her head as she stared steadfastly upwards. She was absolutely still; her bosom scarcely heaved with her breathing. Only her eye moved, seeming to follow some distant object very high above. A crow, or a seagull, or a rabbit, perhaps, thought the corporal. His eye followed the direction of hers, but no living speck broke the stern monotony of the high-piled grassy ridges above, from which glowing torrents of refracted sun-heat rolled downwards upon the couple below. A minute or more passed, Temperance remaining in her absorbed attitude, with thrown-back head and rapt, uplifted gaze; then Ramsall put out his hand and touched her arm. At that touch she started, and seemed to wake.

"Why, Tempy, what had come to you? Asleep and dreaming on your feet? You looked like it!"

He passed his arm round her waist, slightly flat, as the waist of a slim, uncorseted girl of eighteen should be, and drew her fondly to him. But she leaned away with averted eyes, crying softly—

"Oh, Ramsall! didn't you see?"

"See? Nothing but sky, and grass, and you." He pulled her coaxingly, but she still held from him.

"Ramsall, you're making game of me. You mid ha' seen him above on th' bank, right at th' top of th' castle. A long, shining spear in his hand, and something else upon his head, that shone—bright and brazen like the firemen's helmets I've seen hanging up in Chyme Town Hall. And a round shield such as Goliath carries in the Bible pictures—and—"

"Go on, Tempy," the corporal said, with laughter playing about the corners of his well-trimmed moustache and in his bright blue eyes. "Say as 'twere one of th' old Romans come to life and doing sentry-go up there on the top o' the glacis."

But Temperance's lip quivered in awe and not in mirth, and the dark eyes she turned upon the handsome face of the corporal were strained and fearful.

"I mid say it," she answered, "but I daren't; I should be daunted." Intense as was the heat of the noon she shivered, and the corporal laughed outright.

157

"I believe you really think you have seen a ghost. 'Tis a new view of yourself, Temperance, you have given me . . . But I do believe all women are superstitious—believers in signs and omens. With one 'tis a wood-beetle tapping in the clock-case; with another a charming o' bees in the hive, when all by rights should be still; with another a winding-sheet in the candle, or a mysterious knock at the door. With you, 'tis a full-sized ancient Roman with a helmet, spear, and shield, and one who appears, moreover, at full noonday."

The corporal sent his voice out and upwards, and the ringing shout seemed to strike against the overhanging line of the fortifications like something palpable thrown from the hand.

"Halloa!" he shouted. "Halloa, there, you on guard! Challenge the relief and come down for a bit, old fellow, and pass the time o' day." He pretended to listen with cocked ear, and then his expression changed, and he started. "By the Lord! the soldier," he said doubtfully to himself; "if *I* were superstitious I should say that—"

"That somebody answered," whispered a voice close to his ear. It was Temperance's voice, and she was quivering in every limb as she clung to the corporal's strong arm. "Oh, Ramsall—*he did!* I heard him just as you . . . Oh, Ramsall!" Her throbbing heart beat close to the corporal's; her fragrant breath came and went about his face as she panted softly. "It may be . . . a warning of something to come. He wer' sent to give it. Oh, Ramsall!" And so infectious were her alarm and belief that for a moment it seemed to the corporal that high above on the topmost rampart the sunrays were reflected from the shining surface of burnished brass and steel, and that the shadow of a human form slanted blackly downwards over the sun-dried grass. And then he recovered himself, and half-leading, half-supporting Temperance, he passed with her out of the line of the outermost trenches, and there upon the hillside the homely, every-day world was theirs again. As they drew in the salt breeze that puffed from seawards, and looked out together upon the ruby and silver and sapphire of the sunset that follows a hazy day of heat, gulls were busily fishing, their white wings tinged with the red of the sky, and as one persistent bird followed the movements of an unseen fish, turning and winding and diving in the clear, balmy air as its prey did in the denser element, Temperance watched the bird with a tear in her eye.

" 'Tis so my heart mid be following you, Ramsall, when you be away fighting in South Africa!" she said, heaving a great sigh and letting the tear fall.

"Maybe we shan't have the luck to get within shot of the enemy at all," rejoined the corporal; "like the —*th* and the —*th*, that had to squint in the illustrated papers sent from England to see what a Boer looked like."

"But even then you will be fighting the climate," said the dejected girl, "and the water that poisons men and beasts. Oh, Ramsall! 'tis hard to my love to let you go, not knowing surely whether I shall ever see you again."

"It's a poor love that would make a coward of a man that has taken the oath to serve under the colours in peace or in war," said Ramsall, pulling his brown moustache.

"A coward! You a coward, when you dived off the Chyme cliff at high tide in midwinter to save little Freddy Dorley!" cried the girl with swelling heart.

"I had no sweetheart hanging to my coat tails, crying, 'You may stave in your head or ribs against a sunken rock, Ramsall, or at least catch a cold or rheumatism, that may lay you up a cripple, instead of living to be stabbed with a Bridport dagger,' as they used to say in the days when the town was a hemp-market. So I jumped—and the Queen is the richer for it by a soldier this week, for Freddy has taken the shilling."

"Oh! what will his poor old mother say?" cried Temperance.

"Nothing more than you have said or will say. Women's fuss is like the cuckoo-spit on the green leaves in July—a vast deal of froth and spume about a very little matter. Come, Temperance." The corporal was getting tired of dolorous meanings. "Pull yourself together, lass, and be cheerful, and let me see a dry eye when I take train for Plymouth, and I'll make you a promise, on the honour of a soldier."

"And what will the promise be?" asked Temperance, already beginning to bite her lip and choke back her sobs.

" 'Tis this: if 'e have the courage to accept it." The corporal was not smiling now, and his face was grave and earnest. "Face about and give me your hands here, in mine." Holding his sweetheart's hands firmly in his own, and with his blue eyes fixed upon her brown ones, Ramsall Cane repeated: "I, Ramsall Cane, corporal in the Barsetshire Regiment, being under orders for active service at the seat of war, do hereby solemnly promise my intended wife, Temperance Upwey, that be I dead or living, she shall see my face again on earth, walk with me, talk with me, and feel my touch as she does now. So help me God. Amen!"

"Amen!" a deep, hollow voice responded out of space. The lovers paled and started, but the corporal did not loose Temperance's hands.

"We have a witness, it seems," he said, "and all the better, for I mean to keep my oath. Do you keep my conditions and let us have no more tears!"

"I will! I will! only come back living—living!" Temperance moaned, sinking on his broad breast. "How could I bear to lose 'e, my own dear love?"

II.

Ramsall's short furlough came to an end, and Temperance kissed her lover good-bye without shedding a tear. That strange promise of the corporal's had strengthened and consoled her, I do not pretend to explain how. The Barsetshire Regiment sailed for South Africa—and did not once have to look in the English illustrated papers to see what the Boers were like. Of war, hideous and splendid, noble and brutal, glorious and squalid, the Barsetshires had more than their share.

At the Passage of the Tugela a battalion of the regiment crept with three others through the scrub at the foot of the hills towards the ferry. In the first line of skirmishers, twenty feet intervening between man and man, was Corporal Cane. And when the ferry punt was reached and the approaches to the Wagon Drift, the single figure that began to wade across, carrying a line, was the corporal's. Two or three others followed. Then a long chain of men, men with locked arms, a string of human spider-monkeys, entered the yellow turbid current, struggled slowly across and formed up under the shelter of the farther bank. And thus the four infantry battalions crossed, under the silent, deadly observation of the Boers, and a long cloud of dust rose up in the direction of Springfield—and the army was upon the move. Night came down upon that panorama— the living stream of artillery, ammunition-columns, supply-columns, baggage, cattle for commissariat, the thirty great pontoons looking like Brobdingnagian coffins, and the white-tilted, red-crossed ambulances, rolling recklessly, steadily, towards the sound of the unseen water; and from above a deluge of rain poured as though the very skies were weeping over the failure of carefully-laid but futile plans, the retreat to ensue and the slaughter to come, when upon the fatal 24th of January, General Woodgate started from his camp with the Lancashire Fusiliers, the Royal Lancaster Regiment, the Barsetshires, and Thorneycroft's Mounted Infantry; and, under the guidance of Colonel Thorneycroft, made his way up the southern spur of Spion Kop, determined to shell the Boer trenches under cover of the darkness, entrench as far as possible before dawn, hold up the position during the day, drag the guns up at night, and thus dominate the enemy's lines. The story of that splendid struggle, has it not been graven as with a bayonet's point, branded as by fire, upon the hearts of Englishmen and Englishwomen? Little need to expatiate upon the glorious endurance, the dogged bravery displayed by the English regiments throughout the long hours of hellish torment; the pitiless shell-fire, that turned the crowded summit of the "look-out" into a gory, reeking shambles. At four o'clock an English war correspondent rode, with an officer of the —*th* Hussars, to the base of the mountain road, defying the pelting of the storm of death in their anxiety to ascertain the true state of things. Dismounting, they climbed the spur, battling against a human torrent that rolled down from the heights—a torrent of bleeding, blackened, shell-shattered men. Two hundred and nine had passed, some raving in the delirium of thirst and pain, others staggering like drunken men in the intoxication of battle. And upon the heels of these came a tall corporal of the Barsetshires, carrying the body of a young trooper of the Mounted Infantry.

"I know him—I know that poor fellow," said the Hussar afterwards. "He was in the fourth form at Harrow when I left, shot through the head this morning, and only joined last night. Poor chap! Poor little chap!"

"There was no other wound in him except the blue bullet-hole in the temple. It seems his people were

Barsetshire county folk—the Crofts, of Upchyme—and the corporal had known him, too."

"He—the corporal—laid the body down upon a flat rock, and then we saw—well, that half his own ribs on the left side were shot away . . . Odd, but he scarcely seemed to know it, and when I said, 'You're badly wounded, my man!' he put his hand to his side, and brought it away covered with blood, and stared at it in a surprised kind of way. And then he said something about keeping a promise, and staggered from us, and went tipping and blundering down the rocky path, stumbling at every step. A little lower down he fell—and didn't get up again. But it was he who'd saved Calderwood's life in the fight on the summit, and he, again, who was the first man to cross the Tugela. And he'd have had a commission if he'd got through. But it's the luck of war! And I wondered, after, what was that promise he was so set on keeping, dead or alive, poor beggar! Something to do with a woman, I dare say!"

Something to do with a woman! At five o'clock the brave corporal had fallen and died, at five o'clock the gate of Mrs. Upwey's little fenced-in garden clicked, and Temperance, knitting on the doorstep with a shawl about her to ward off the nipping January breeze, looked up and saw, with a sudden terrible convulsion of her whole being, the head and shoulders of a soldier in khaki leaning over by the berried holly bush. No doubt as to whom those merry blue eyes—hollower and larger than they used to be—belonged. A stubby beard disfigured his handsome chin, his face was deeply bronzed and haggard with toil and privation, and his khaki uniform was blackened and torn, especially upon the left side; but it was Ramsall— her Ramsall; and she leapt to her feet as the little gate swung open, and fell speechlessly upon her lover's breast.

He stroked her hair with his thin brown hand and clasped her to him and kissed her, and the kiss and the clasp were very warm and real. Measureless content overflooded her, her soul brimmed at her lips. She looked up at him with eyes that worshipped, and could not speak for bliss . . . Then she stammered.

"The—the surprise! 'Tis too great—too joyful, almost. Th' war cannot be over!" He smiled. "Nay—you have been invalided home!" Her voice grew shrill with terror. "Oh, Ramsall—you have been wounded!"

"Ay, ay, maid," the corporal said, still stroking her hair. "I was wounded."

"But you're right now?" she asked anxiously.

"All's well with me now, thank God!" There was a deeper tenderness in his manner than Temperance had ever been sensible of before.

"Come in," she said, "come in, and speak to mother."

"Eh! my sweetheart alive," screamed Mrs. Upwey, when Temperance led her recovered lover in. "Ramsall Cane travelled back athirt seas wi'out as much as 'by your leave' or 'with your pleasure'!"

"They said that I might come, Mrs. Upwey," the corporal replied, standing grave and straight and tall in the middle of the little cottage house-place, with the flicker of the wood fire snatching gleams from his buttons and belt-buckle.

"Anan?" said the widow, blankly.

"He means the military authorities, mother," explained Temperance, proud of her superior knowledge.

"And have you been in real actual battle?" asked Mrs. Upwey.

"Ay, real battle," replied the soldier. "But now my fighting's over. Rest from henceforth, for me!"

His blue eyes looked through the open door towards the fading sunset, and there was a smile upon his lips that Tempy never forgot.

"Shut the door, Tempy," ordered the girl's mother, bustling to her little pantry-hutch. "D'ye want the lad to be all afroze comin' out o' they hot countries? And you, Ramsall, mid sit down and ate a bit. A dish o' vried eggs an' rashers, such as 'e used to be vond of, an' a cup o' tay."

"I thank you, mother, but I'll neither eat nor drink," the corporal said quietly, "that is, not now, not here. Thy maid," he laid a hand on the shoulder of Temperance, and her blood ran warm at the bliss-giving touch—"Temperance, will come wi' me for a stroll. We'll go as far as the castle and there part."

"Why," Temperance cried out in bitter disappointment, "must you go away to-night?"

"Ay," said the corporal, "for I'm not spared for long, I must be back at Headquarters by the time they said."

"They are cruel, heartless folk, then!" burst out Temperance, with flashing eyes and panting bosom; but a look she had never seen before came into her lover's eyes, and at his imperative gesture for silence, she complained no more.

And they went from the humble cottage together into the biting cold of the January afternoon, and climbed the steep narrow pathway, now lightly powdered with snow. Temperance was blissfully content for the time being . . .

Her hand was in Ramsall's. He had said there would be no more fighting for him. She had a vision of a home—hers and his—and of two lives spent in wedded union crowned with sweet and common joys.

Suddenly she spoke, as the outworks of the old Roman fortress rose into sight.

"There is the clump of thyme!" She pointed to a tuft of withered stalks. "We raced to it the last day we were here together, and I won. Now we walk soberly hand in hand. I pray that we may walk so through life together."

The corporal smiled, looking up at the reddening sunset, and they passed between the frosted banks of short grass into the first enclosure of the castle.

"Here a friend waits for me," said the voice Temperance loved, "and here, my love, we kiss and part. For I must leave you."

"Not for long!" cried Temperance wildly. "Oh, Ramsall, not for very long!"

As she moved towards the corporal, with hands held out in entreaty, he stepped back, and so strange was the expression of the blue eyes and the handsome soldierly features, that the girl drew back.

"Are you angry with me, dearest?" she asked, trembling.

For answer the corporal smiled and shook his head, and then, in an instant, Temperance stood alone in a wintry sunset, under the frowning grass ramparts that towered overhead.

"Ramsall!" she cried. "Oh, not for long!" and a cry came back from high overhead.

"Not for long!"

It was Ramsall's voice, she knew. She threw back her head and stared upwards . . . Sharply outlined against the wintry sunset sky, upon the extreme summit of the castle, stood the figures of two men, alike in soldierly height and proportion, strangely different in dress. For one wore a gleaming brazen helmet, breastplate and greaves, and carried a spear with a broad, shining blade, and the other was an English infantryman in the stained and ragged khaki of Active Service. As Temperance looked, the figures stood there together, strong, soldierly and serene; and as she looked again, they vanished from her sight, and the heart of the mystery was laid bare to her, in one lightning flash of comprehension.

"Ramsall is dead! He kept his promise, came to me, and now has gone again," a voice said in her heart.

She was bowed like an aged woman as she went homewards.

"Ramsall is dead," she said to her mother, when Mrs. Upwey met her at the cottage door. And the following night brought a letter from a friend in Chyme, containing a page of the local daily paper that told the story of the gallant corporal's death. Day dawned as the mother and daughter spelt out the last words.

"But he kept his promise," Temperance whispered. "And he said our parting would not be for long."

Nor was it.

Miss Clo Graves at Home

"Were it for any other paper in the world than *The Gentlewoman* I wouldn't have let you come at all," said Miss Clo Graves, as I settled myself for a chat in her pleasant studio, which is situated in a quaint dip off an airy road within sight of Primrose-hill. "You would never believe what I've suffered from the irresponsible interviewer! Usually he begins something in this style:—'Miss Clo Graves is a bright and intellectual Irishwoman. She arrived alone and unprotected in this country with eleven little brothers and sisters under one arm, and a red herring under the other as her sole means of support. After unheard-of privations and a heroic struggle with the realities of life she has attained—' *et cetera.* And hardly a word of truth in the whole of it."

Somewhat staggered at this trenchant view of my really quite innocuous tribe, I hastened to inquire what the real facts of my hostess's experiences were.

Her first literary effort was made very early in life. "Only the other day," she said, "I found in a forgotten drawer the worn-out manuscript of a burlesque version of the *Idylls of the King* that I wrote when I was twelve. We acted it, I and my brothers and sisters, in a big garret that we used to play in; but I never had much chance in our theatricals, because an ambitious sister always took all the best parts."

With some hesitation, I asked what happened when Miss Graves's family left Ireland.

"Now you're getting dangerously near the eleven brothers and sisters and the bloater," laughed Miss Clo Graves, to whom a blue and gold Japanese kimono proved remarkably becoming. "However, I'll confide to you that the well-known Bishop of Limerick is the head of the family and that my father was a soldier. At one time, his regiment being stationed in Southsea, we resided in that town, and it is the manners and customs of the girls there that I have burlesqued in *The Mother of Three*—you remember the place is called Rocksea in the play. Later on we lived in the Isle of Wight, and eventually removed to London for the sake of my artistic education."

"You began life as an art student?"

"Yes, black and white work, at Queen-square School, and paid my own expenses there by working for *Fun* and *Judy*. There was a time when I wrote three pages of *Fun* weekly—mostly burlesquing new stories; I used also to design little grotesque illustrations to my own work in pen and ink outline."

Of editors—that much-maligned race—Miss Clo Graves speaks most warmly. The courtesy she has always received from them, she declares, has made her work a pleasure, while to the kindly criticism and wise counsel of Mr. Clement Scott and Mr. Alfred Watson, under whose editorship she worked some years ago, she considers herself very greatly indebted. Magazine writing has, of course, long claimed her for its own, as witness her admirable serial now running in *The Gentlewoman*, and the innumerable stories and articles she has contributed to *The World*, *The St. James's Gazette*, *The Sporting and Dramatic*, and, indeed, to nearly all the leading weeklies. At one time she even edited a daily column in an afternoon paper, and anyone who has ever done that will know what it means.

After spending some time in studying at the Queen-square School of Art, Miss Clo Graves tried her luck on the stage, and for four or five years threw in her lot with stock companies and provincial tours, in the course of which experience a probably unique offer was made to her. She was asked to undertake the responsibilities of assistant stage manager of a burlesque company—an honour she gratefully declined.

"Now, tell me," I entreated, "about your plays, the technical excellencies of which you have already, to some extent, accounted for."

"Well," responded the author of them, "as to *The Mother of Three*—which by the bye I wrote in six weeks—I have already had six applications for the acting rights from America, four from Australia, eight from the English provinces, three from Germany, one from Austria, and one from Italy, not to mention the negotiations which are now in progress for the production of the play in Paris. The idea is, I think, original inasmuch as it was not derived from the French, or, indeed, taken from anybody! Indeed, I may say my Triplets have broken new ground; the little sketch, 'Husband Hunting', which I wrote for *The Gentlewoman* at Christmas being the only other use I have ever made of the idea of three poor girls going out by turns in a single evening gown."

"The first play I ever wrote was *Nitocris*, which was produced at Drury Lane in 1887. I was then working in London, and was especially engaged in writing pantomime lyrics for Sir Augustus Harris's use. He by chance discovering that I had lying by in a cupboard a poetical play of my own in five acts, generously offered the use of Drury Lane Theatre and the scenery of the opera *Aïda* for the matinée. This I was able to arrange for, and *Nitocris* was duly performed, the late Miss Sophie Eyre playing with magnificent effect the leading part."

The next theatrical venture in which Miss Clo Graves was interested was a dramatic version of Rider Haggard's

She, to which Mr. Edward Rose had already written a prologue when she was asked to collaborate with him. This she accordingly did, and the result was moderately successful.

After this came *Rachel*, a one-act poetical play produced at a series of matinées at the Haymarket Theatre. And then, alas! Miss Clo Graves fell ill from overwork, and for seventeen weeks was prostrate with brain fever. During this long illness she was attended by a most clever physician whose character afterwards furnished the personality of Dr. Neill in the play of that name. "Indeed," says the author, "*Dr. and Mrs. Neill* was written as a testimony of gratitude to the medical profession." In 1891 the Kendals took *Katharine Kavanagh*—a three-act drama adapted by Miss Graves in collaboration with Mrs. Oscar Beringer from Miss Graves's successful novel *Dragon's Teeth*—on tour through the United States, and in 1893 came the production by Mr. Augustin Daly of a one-act German mediaeval play, entitled *The Knave*, at Daly's Theatre, New York. The part of *Mockworld* was created by that greatest of comedians, Miss Ada Rehan, and the piece met with an enthusiastic reception from public and press.

"And the next production?" I ventured. "Of course you are writing a new play. Is it indiscreet to ask after it?"

"*Very*," responded my hostess, "and I shall only tell you that it will be a Society comedy, and that I am collaborating with another writer—a woman—in its production." And with this meagre information I had perforce to content myself.

And then my hostess drew my attention to curios and the many quaint Chinese and Japanese articles which adorn the walls of the studio, and which have been sent home by her brother, Captain Graves, of the Chinese Imperial Service, who was one of the famous five Europeans who

fought in the great naval battle before Wei-hai-wei. In the
hall, as I departed, I was confronted by a huge wooden slab
to be erected in the garden to the memory of "Boojum, a
faithful little cat", a black Persian which for long was the
presiding genius of the studio on Primrose Hill.

Alias Richard Dehan

Grant Overton

I.

At that, I think I am wrong. I think the title of this chapter ought to be "Alias Clotilde Graves".

The problems of literary personality are strange. Some time after the Boer War a woman who had been in newspaper work in London and who had even, at one time, been on the stage under the necessity of earning her living, wrote a novel. The novel happened to be an intensive study of the Boer War, made possible by the fact that the writer was the daughter of a soldier and had spent her early years in barracks. England at that time was interested by the subject of this novel. It sold largely and its author was established by the book.

She was forty-six years old in the year when the book was published. But this was not the striking thing. William De Morgan produced the first of his impressive novels at a much more advanced age. The significant thing was that in publishing her novel, *The Dop Doctor* [1910] (American title: *One Braver Thing*), Clotilde Graves chose the pen name of Richard Dehan, although she was already known as a writer (chiefly for the theatre) under her own name.

I do not know that Miss Graves has ever said anything publicly about her motive in electing the name of Richard

Dehan. But I feel that whatever the cause the result was the distinct emergence of a totally different personality. There is no final disassociation between Clotilde Graves and Richard Dehan. Richard Dehan, novelist, steadily employs the material furnished in valuable abundance by Clotilde Graves's life. At the same time the personality of Richard Dehan is so unusual, so gifted, so lavish in its invention and so much at home in surprising backgrounds, that something approaching a psychic explanation of authorship seems called for.

II.

Clotilde Inez Mary Graves was born at Barracks, Buttevant, County Cork, Ireland, on June 3, 1864, third daughter of the late Major W. H. Graves of the Eighteenth Royal Irish Regiment and Antoinette, daughter of Captain George Anthony Deane of Harwich. Thus, the English *Who's Who*.

"She numbers among her ancestors admirals and deans," said *The Bookman* in 1912.

As the same magazine at about the same time spoke of her as descended from Charles II's naval architect, Admiral Sir Anthony Deane, one wonders if Sir Anthony were not the sum of the admirals and the total of the deans. But no; at any rate in so far as the admirals are concerned, for Miss Graves is also said to be distantly related to Admiral Nelson.

I will give you what *The Bookman* said in the "Chronicle and Comment" columns of its number for February 1913:

Richard Dehan was nine years old when her family emigrated to England from their Irish home. She had seen a good deal of barrack life, and at Southsea, where they went to live, she acquired a large knowledge of both services in the circle of naval and military friends they made there, and this knowledge years afterward she turned to account in *Between Two Thieves*. In 1884, Miss Graves became an art student and worked at the British Museum galleries and the Royal Female School of Art, helping to support herself by journalism of a lesser kind, among other things drawing little pen-and-ink grotesques for the comic papers. By and by she resolved to take to dramatic writing and being too poor, she says, to manage in any other way, she abandoned art and took an engagement in a travelling theatrical company. In 1888 her first chance as a dramatist came. She was again in London, working vigorously at journalism, when some one was needed to write extra lyrics for a pantomime then in preparation. A letter of recommendation from an editor to the manager ended in Miss Clo Graves writing the pantomime of *Puss in Boots*. Later a tragedy by her, *Nitocris*, was produced for an afternoon at Drury Lane, and another of her plays, *The Mother of Three*, proved not only a literary, but also a material, success.

Her first novel to be signed Richard Dehan being so successful, an English publisher planned to bring out an earlier, minor work, already published as by Clotilde Graves, with "Richard Dehan" on the title-page. The author was stirred to a vigorous and public protest. In the ensuing controversy someone made the point that the proposed reissue would not be more indefensible than the act of a publishing house in bringing out posthumous "books" by O. Henry and dragging from its deserved oblivion Rudyard Kipling's *Abaft the Funnel*.

A Vanished Hand

I do not know whether the publishing of books is a
business or a profession. I should say that it has, at one time
or another and by one or another individual or concern,
been pursued as either or both.

There have certainly been, and probably are, book
publishers who not only conduct their business as a
business but as a business of a low order. There have been
and are book publishers who, though quite necessarily
business men, observe an ethical code as nice as that of any
of the recognised professions. Perhaps publishing books
should qualify as an art, since it has the characteristics
of bringing out what is best or worst in a publisher; and,
indeed, if we are to hold that any successful means of self-
expression is art, then publishing books has been an art
more than once; for unquestionably there are publishers
who find self-expression in their work.

This is an interesting subject, but I must not pursue it in
this place. Certainly Miss Graves was justified in objecting
to the use of her new pen name on work already published
under her own name. In her case, as I think, the objection
was peculiarly well-founded, because it seems to me that
Richard Dehan was a new person. Since Richard Dehan
appeared on the title-page of *The Dop Doctor*, there has
never been a Clotilde Graves in books. You have only to
study the books. The *Dop Doctor* was followed, two years
later, by *Between Two Thieves*. This novel has as a leading
character Florence Nightingale under the name of Ada
Merling. The story was at first to have been called *The Lady
with the Lamp*; but the author delayed it for a year and
subjected it to a complete rewriting, the result of a new and
enlarged conception of the story.

Then came a steady succession of novels by Richard
Dehan. I remember with what surprise I read, in 1918,
That Which Hath Wings, a war story of large dimensions

178

and an incredible amount of exact and easy detail. I
remember, too, noting that there was embedded in it a
marvellous story for children—an airplane flight in which
a youngster figured—if the publisher chose, with the
author's consent, to lift this out of its larger, adult setting.
I remember very vividly reading in 1920 a collection of
short stories by Richard Dehan, published under the title
The Eve of Pascua. Pascua is the Spanish word for Easter. I
wondered where on earth, unless in Spain itself, the author
got the bright colouring for his story.

What I did not realise at the time was that Richard Dehan
is like that. Now, smitten to earth by the 500-page novel
which he has just completed, I think I understand better.
The Just Steward, from one standpoint, makes the labours of
Gustave Flaubert in *Salammbô* seem trivial. It is known with
what passionate tenacity and surprising ardour the French
master studied the subject of ancient Carthage, grubbing
like the lowliest archaeologist to get at his fingertips all
those recondite allusions so necessary if he were to move
with lightness, assurance and consummate art through the
scenes of his novel. But, frankly, one does not expect this of
the third daughter of an Irish soldier, an ex-journalist and
the author of a Drury Lane pantomime. Nevertheless the
erudition is all here. From this standpoint, *The Just Steward*
is truly monumental. I will show you a sample or two:

> Beautiful, even with the trench and wall of
> Diocletian's comparatively recent siege scarring the
> orchards and vineyards of Lake Mareotis, splendid
> even though her broken canals and aqueducts had
> never been repaired, and part of her western quarter
> still displayed heaps of calcined ruins where had
> been temples, palaces and academies, Alexandria lay
> shimmering under the African sun . . . .

The vintage of Egypt was in full swing, the figs and dates were being harvested. Swarms of wasps and hornets, armed with formidable stings, yellow-striped like the dreaded nomads of the south and eastern frontiers, greedily sucked the sugary juices of the ripe fruit. Flocks of fig-birds twittered amongst the branches, being like the date-pigeons, almost too gorged to fly. Half naked, dark or tawny skinned, tattooed native labourers, hybrids of mingled races, with heads close-shaven save for a topknot, dwellers in mud-hovels, drudges of the water-wheel, cut down the heavy grape-clusters with sickle-shaped cooper knives.

Ebony, woolly-haired negroes in clean white breech-cloths, piled up the gathered fruit in tall baskets woven of reeds and lined with leaves. Copts with the rich reddish skins, the long eyes and boldly curving profiles of Egyptian warriors and monarchs as presented on the walls of ancient temples of Libya and the Thebaïd, moved about in leather-girdled blue linen tunics and hide sandals, keeping account of the laden panniers, roped upon the backs of diminutive asses and carried to the winepresses as fast as they were filled.

The negroes sang as they set snares for fig-birds, and stuffed themselves to the throat with grapes and custard-apples. The fat beccaficoes beloved of the epicurean fell by hundreds into the limed horsehair traps. Greek, Egyptian and negro girls, laughing under garlands of hibiscus, periwinkle and tuberoses, coaxed the fat morsels out of the black men to carry home for a supper treat, while acrobats, comic singers, sellers of cakes, drinks and sweetmeats, with strolling jugglers and jesters and

Jewish fortune-tellers of both sexes, assailed the workers and the merrymakers with importunities and made harvest in their own way.

The story is extraordinary. Opening in the Alexandria of the fourth century, it pictures two men, a Roman official and a Jewish steward, who are friends unto death. The second of the four parts or books into which the novel is divided opens in England in 1914. We have to do with John Hazel, the descendant of Hazaël Aben Hazaël, and with the lovely Katharine Forbis, whose ancestor was a Roman, Hazaël Aben Hazaël's sworn friend.

A story of exciting action certainly; it has elements that would ordinarily be called melodramatic—events which are focussed down into realities against the tremendous background of an incredible war. The exotic settings are Egypt and Palestine. It must not be thought that the story is bizarre; the scenes in England, the English slang of John Hazel, as well as the typical figure of Trixie, Lady Wastwood, are utterly modern. I do not find anything to explain how Miss Graves could write such a book; the answer is that Richard Dehan wrote it.

III.

Miss Graves, of whose antecedents and education we already know something, is a Roman Catholic in faith and a Liberal Unionist in politics. She lives at The Towers, Beeding, near Bramber, Sussex. Her recreations are gardening and driving.

But Richard Dehan knows the early history of the Christian Church; he knows military life, strategy, tactics, types; he knows in a most extraordinary way the details of Jewish history and religious observances; he knows perfectly and as a matter of course all about English middle class life; he knows all sorts of things about the East—Turkey and Arabia and those countries.

This is a discrepancy which will bear a good deal of accounting for.

[At this point, the author digresses to quote another lengthy excerpt from The Just Steward, *before returning to the point he had just made. – ed.]*

IV.

[. . . .]

If you receive a letter from The Towers, Beeding, it will bear a double signature, like this:

RICHARD DEHAN
CLOTILDE GRAVES

Clotilde Graves has become a secondary personality.

There was once a time when there was no Richard Dehan. There now are times when there is no Clotilde Graves.

To a woman in middle age an opportunity presented itself. It was the chance to write a novel around the subject which, as a girl, she had come to know a great deal about— the subject of war. To write about it and gain attention, the novel required a man's signature.

Then there was born in the mind of the woman who purposed to write the novel the idea of a man—of *the* man—who should be the novelist she wanted to be. He should use as by right and from instinct the material which lay inutile at her woman's disposal.

She created Richard Dehan. Perhaps, in so doing, she created another monster like Frankenstein's. I do not know.

Born of necessity and opportunity and a woman's inventiveness, Richard Dehan took over whatever of Clotilde Graves's he could use. He is now the master. It is, intellectually and spiritually, as if he were the full-grown son of Clotilde Graves. It is a partnership not less intimate than that.

Clotilde Graves—but she does not matter. I think she existed to bring Richard Dehan into the world.

Sources

"How the Mistress Came Home" was collected in *The Cost of Wings and Other Stories* (Heinemann, 1914).

"A Spirit Elopement" was collected in *Off Sandy Hook and Other Stories* (Heinemann, 1915).

"Lilium Peccatorum" was collected in *Earth to Earth* (Heinemann, 1916).

"A Vanished Hand" was collected in *The Cost of Wings and Other Stories* (Heinemann, 1914); it also appeared in *Bending to Earth: Strange Stories by Irish Women* edited by Maria Giakaniki and Brian J. Showers (Swan River Press, 2019).

"Lady Clanbevan's Baby" was collected in *Off Sandy Hook and Other Stories* (Heinemann, 1915).

"Peter" was collected in *Under the Hermés and Other Stories* (Heinemann, 1917).

"Clairvoyance" was collected in *The Headquarter Recruit and Other Stories* (Heinemann, 1913).

"The Compleat Housewife" appeared under the name "Clotilde Graves" in *The Windsor Magazine* (February 1910); it was collected in *Under the Hermés and Other Stories* (Heinemann, 1917).

"The Mother of Turquoise" appeared under the name "Clotilde Graves" in *The London Magazine* (March 1907); it was collected in *The Eve of Pascua and Other Stories* (Heinemann, 1920).

"The Tooth of Tuloo" was collected in *Under the Hermés and Other Stories* (Heinemann, 1917).

"The Great Beast of Kafue" was collected in *Under the Hermés and Other Stories* (Heinemann, 1917).

"The Friend" was collected in *The Man with the Mask and Other Stories* (Heinemann, 1931).

"Dark Dawn" was collected in *The Man with the Mask and Other Stories* (Heinemann, 1931).

"Miss Clo Graves at Home" was first published in *The Gentlewoman* (2 May 1896).

"Alias Richard Dehan" by Grant Overton was collected in *When Winter Comes to Main Street* (George H. Doran Company, 1922).

Acknowledgements

I would like to thank Brian J. Showers of Swan River Press for commissioning this volume of stories and for his continuing commitment to republishing the work of Irish women writers. The editor and publisher would also like to express their thanks to Brian Coldrick, Timothy J. Jarvis, Meggan Kehrli, Jim Rockhill and Steve J. Shaw for their assistance in the compilation and production of this volume, the first to showcase the imaginitive fiction of Clotide Graves. I would also like to thank Jeff Makala for his feedback on the introduction. As always, my gratitude goes to Murray, Maggie, Kitsey, and Remy for their furry support.

About the Author

Clotilde Graves (1863-1932) was born in Co. Cork on 3 June 1863. Often unconventional and uncompromising, she not only adopted a male pseudonym, but male dress and manners as well. Under the name "Richard Dehan", she wrote historical novels and several collections of short stories. Her popular novel *The Dop Doctor* found further success on the silver screen in 1915. Graves retired in 1928 to a convent in Hatch End, Middlesex, where she died on 3 December 1932.

About the Editor

Melissa Edmundson specialises in nineteenth and early twentieth-century British women writers, with a particular interest in women's supernatural fiction. She is author of *Women's Ghost Literature in Nineteenth-Century Britain* (2013) and *Women's Colonial Gothic Writing, 1850-1930: Haunted Empire* (2018). Her anthologies include *Women's Weird: Strange Stories by Women, 1890-1940* (2019), *Women's Weird 2: More Strange Stories by Women, 1891-1937* (2020), and a collection of Elinor Mordaunt's fiction, *The Villa and The Vortex: Supernatural Stories, 1916-1924* (2021).

SWAN RIVER PRESS

Founded in 2003, Swan River Press is an independent publishing company, based in Dublin, Ireland, dedicated to gothic, supernatural, and fantastic literature. We specialise in limited edition hardbacks, publishing fiction from around the world with an emphasis on Ireland's contributions to the genre.

www.swanriverpress.ie

"Handsome, beautifully made volumes . . .
altogether irresistible."

– Michael Dirda, *Washington Post*

"It [is] often down to small, independent, specialist presses
to keep the candle of horror fiction flickering . . . "

– Darryl Jones, *Irish Times*

"Swan River Press has emerged as one of the most inspiring
new presses over the past decade. Not only are the books
beautifully presented and professionally produced, but they
aspire consistently to high literary quality and originality,
ranging from current writers of supernatural/weird fiction
to rare or forgotten works by departed authors."

– Peter Bell, *Ghosts & Scholars*

BENDING TO EARTH
Strange Stories by Irish Women

edited by Maria Giakaniki
and Brian J. Showers

Irish women have long produced literature of the gothic, uncanny, and supernatural. *Bending to Earth* draws together twelve such tales. While none of the authors herein were considered primarily writers of fantastical fiction during their lifetimes, they each wandered at some point in their careers into more speculative realms—some only briefly, others for lengthier stays.

Names such as Charlotte Riddell and Rosa Mulholland will already be familiar to aficionados of the eerie, while Katharine Tynan and Clotilde Graves are sure to gain new admirers. From a ghost story in the Swiss Alps to a premonition of death in the West of Ireland to strange rites in a South Pacific jungle, *Bending to Earth* showcases a diverse range of imaginative writing which spans the better part of a century.

"Bending to Earth *is full of tales of women walled-up in rooms, of vengeful or unforgetting dead wives, of mistreated lovers, of cruel and murderous husbands.*"

– Darryl Jones, *Irish Times*

"*A surprising, extraordinary anthology featuring twelve uncanny and supernatural stories from the nineteenth century . . . highly recommended, extremely enjoyable.*"

– *British Fantasy Society*

"NUMBER NINETY"

& Other Ghost Stories

B. M. Croker

The bestselling Irish author B. M. Croker enjoyed a highly successful literary career from 1880 until her death forty years later. Her novels were witty and fast moving, set mostly in India and her native Ireland. Titles such as *Proper Pride* (1882) and *Diana Barrington* (1888) found popularity for their mix of romantic drama and Anglo-Indian military life. And, like many late-Victorian authors, Croker also wrote ghost stories for magazines and Christmas annuals. From the colonial nightmares such as "The Dâk Bungalow at Dakor" and "The North Verandah" to the more familiar streets of haunted London in "Number Ninety", this collection showcases fifteen of B. M. Croker's most effective supernatural tales.

"This is a solid collection of stories that deserve to be better known . . . they are all enjoyable ghostly tales, and ideal reading for the long winter nights."

– Supernatural Tales

"[Croker's] Indian stories evoke colonial life vividly . . . What makes them all readable are the well-observed characters and settings"

– Wormwood

THE DEATH SPANCEL
and Others

Katharine Tynan

Katharine Tynan is not a name immediately associated with the supernatural. However, like many other writers of the early twentieth century, she made numerous forays into literature of the ghostly and macabre, and throughout her career produced verse and prose that conveys a remarkable variety of eerie themes, moods, and narrative forms. From her early, elegiac stories, inspired by legends from the West of Ireland, to pulpier efforts featuring grave-robbers and ravenous rats, Tynan displays an eye for weird detail, compelling atmosphere, and a talent for rendering a broad palette of uncanny effects. *The Death Spancel and Others* is the first collection to showcase Tynan's tales of supernatural events, prophecies, curses, apparitions, and a pervasive sense of the ghastly.

"Of remarkably high literary quality . . . a great collection recommended to any good fiction lover."

– Mario Guslandi

"Tynan's fiction is of a high standard, crafted in relatively simple yet still lyrical prose . . . a very assured craftswoman of the supernatural tale."

– Supernatural Tales

"Lovers of late Victorian and Edwardian ghost fiction will assuredly adore the restrained literary quality . . ."

– The Pan Review